Dray Prescot tells the story of his adventures on Kregen on cassettes which he sends me from time to time during his visits to Earth. He has had a remarkable and varied career on that remarkable and varied world, four hundred light-years away, eventually being elected Emperor of Vallia. Each of the volumes of his story is arranged to be read as an individual book, so although *Werewolves of Kregen* is #33 in the Saga, it can be picked up and read with enjoyment by a reader unfamiliar with the preceding volumes. Of course, familiarity with the fascinating ins and outs of Dray Prescot's story must give greater enjoyment; but, then, a reader coming to the Saga for the first time has that pleasurable satisfaction in store.

The island Empire of Vallia, sundered by internal dissension and invasion, is gradually reestablishing itself. Prescot returns from the island of Pandahem to the south to help in that struggle. *Werewolves of Kregen* is the first book in a new cycle of adventures chronicling that struggle and the beginning of the Nine Unspeakable Curses Against Vallia. Under the streaming mingled lights of the Suns of Scorpio Dray Prescot must go on to whatever fate destiny holds for him.

—*Alan Burt Akers*

The Adventures of Dray Prescot are
narrated in DAW Books:

TRANSIT TO SCORPIO
FIRES OF SCORPIO
MAZES OF SCORPIO
DELIA OF VALLIA
MANHOUNDS/ARENA OF ANTARES
BEASTS OF ANTARES
REBEL OF ANTARES
A LIFE FOR KREGEN
A VICTORY FOR KREGEN
LEGIONS OF ANTARES
TALONS OF SCORPIO
SEG THE BOWMAN
etc.

WEREWOLVES OF KREGEN

by
Dray Prescot

As told to Alan Burt Akers

DAW Books, Inc.
Donald A. Wollheim, Publisher
1633 Broadway, New York, N.Y. 10019

PUBLISHED BY
THE NEW AMERICAN LIBRARY
OF CANADA LIMITED

The Witch War Cycle
Werewolves of Kregen

DAW Collectors' Book No. 611

First Printing, January 1985

2 3 4 5 6 7 8 9

For Simon de Wolfe
and the Hundred Henchfolk.

CONTENTS

CHAPTER ONE

THE FIRST DEATHS

Gray mist parted before the prow of the narrow boat, clung damply to our faces, dewed our evening cloaks with diamonds. Gaunt fingers of mist reached across the canal to the opposite bank where the blank stone rear of a villa patched a mass of darkness against the night.

We were a silent company with only the soft ripple of water as an accompaniment. Then Seg said: "A damned spooky night, this, my old dom."

Seg Segutorio is one of the fey ones of two worlds, and at his words his wife Milsi put her arm through his more securely and pressed closer. Delia responded with one of her silvery-golden laughs and was about to pass a scathing comment on the gullibility of some folk over ghouls and spookies and the Kregen equivalent of things that go bump in the night, when young Fortin, standing in the prow with his boathook, called out.

"Look! On the bank—there!"

We all looked. A man wrapped in a cloak walked unsteadily along the towpath and I was about to inquire with a touch of sarcasm of young Fortin what we were supposed to be staring at when a humped gray mass launched itself through the air.

The man had no chance. Screaming, writhing, he went down into the mud.

A monstrous shaggy shape hunched above him. The impression of crimson eyes, of yellow fangs, of a thick and coarsely tangled pelt, of a beast-form bunched with demonic energy was followed by the clearly heard crunch of bones breaking through.

The people in the narrow boat set up a yelling. The beast reared his head. He stared out full at us. Smoky ruby eyes glared malevolently. The yellow fangs and black jaws glistened thickly with blood that darkened ominously in that uncertain light.

Seg reached around to his back for the great Lohvian long bow that was not there. We were all dressed for the evening's entertainment, with rapiers and left-hand daggers. A lady and gentleman do not normally need longbows and war-swords and shields along the streets and canals of Vondium, the capital of the Empire of Vallia.

Kregen's first Moon, the Maiden with the Many Smiles, cast down her fuzzy pink light upon the slatey waters, and tendrils of mist coiled up to engulf the light. The air darkened.

"Steer for the bank!" I bellowed.

Old Naghan the Tiller put his helm over at once and we glided into the bank. Fortin fended us off and Seg and I leaped ashore.

The poor fellow was dead, his throat torn clean out.

Delia said, "Call the Watch."

"Can you see the damn beast?" Seg glared about.

In the shifting shards of pinkish illumination, with the mist bafflingly obscuring details, we could see no sign of that monstrous shaggy beast.

Dormvelt, the bo'sun, hauled out his silver whistle—it was a whistle and not a pipe—and blew. The City Fathers, instituted by the Presidio to run many of the day-to-day functions of Vondium, had suggested that a City Watch would be in keeping with the requirements of law and order. The Pallans, the ministers or secretaries, responsible for their various departments of Vallia, had agreed. I was pleased now to see how rapidly the Watch tumbled up, summoned by Dormvelt's call.

These were not the happy, rapscallion, lethargic Watch of Sanurkazz, who invariably turned up too late at a fracas, with swords rusted into their scabbards. These men were old soldiers, with stout polearms, and lanterns, and a couple of werstings on leather leashes reinforced with brass.

"What's to do, koters?" called their leader who wore yellow and white feathers in his hat.

Then he saw me.

He knew better than to go into the extravagant full incline, all slavish indignity in a free man.

"Majister!"

"Lahal, Tom the Toes," I said, for I recognized him for an old churgur of the army. As a churgur he still carried sword and shield. His men shone their lanterns on the corpse.

"A bad business. Did you see a monstrous great animal running off?"

"No majister." Tom the Toes rattled his sword against his shield. "Larko! If you can't keep those dratted werstings quiet in the presence of the emperor, then—"

"I dunno, Tom—look at 'em! They're going crazy . . ."

Werstings, those vicious black and white striped hunting dogs, are popularly supposed to be tamed into serving humanity as watchdogs and hunting dogs.

But most folk eye them askance, knowing with that sixth sense of humans that the dogs are only pretending to be tamed and that they will break out into their savage ways at the first opportunity. Now the two werstings were drawing back their lips, exposing their fangs. They were snarling deep in their throats, guttural and menacing sounds. The hair around their necks stood up and their backs bristled.

Larko held onto the leashes, hanging back, and I'd swear that at any moment he'd be towed along with his heels slipping in the mud.

"The beast's scent upsets them," said Delia. "So we follow."

Trust Delia to get to the heart of anything faster than anyone else.

Tom the Toes, holding himself very erect, huffed and puffed, and got out: "Majestrix! My lady! You are not dressed or weaponed for danger—majestrix—"

Delia, who is the Empress of Vallia as well as the lady of many other realms of Kregen, knew exactly the right answer to this tough old soldier.

"You have the right of it, Tom. Therefore you brave lads can go on ahead into the danger, and I will skulk along at the back. Does that please you?"

"Delia!" I said, and looked at Tom, who bit his lip, and then swung about and yelled with great ill-temper upon his men. He was, of course, a Deldar in command of this patrol, and, like all Deldars, he could bellow.

We all set off after the werstings who now that the backward pressure was released from their leashes seemed mightily reluctant to follow the scent that so disturbed them. They started off, and then they stopped, making horrid little noises low down in the scale.

"They won't have it," announced Larko. Now he was trying to pull them along, and they dragged back. "This ain't like my werstings at all—come on, Polly, come on, Fancy. Don't make a fool of me in front o' the emperor and the empress."

But the werstings, it was quite clear, were prepared to make a fool of anybody rather than follow that scent.

We were getting nowhere so I made the obvious decision.

The City Fathers had allocated houses in each precinct to be turned into guardhouses where the patrols of the Watch were based. Since the Time of Troubles, which had torn Vallia into shreds, peoples' lives were vastly different from what they had been in the old prosperous days of peace and plenty. The times bred restless spirits, men and women hardened by suffering who demanded back from anyone available what they considered their due. A Watch even in Vondium was necessary. We had not worn war-gear; the times, wrong though they were, were not as bad as that.

I said, "Tom, better get back to your guardhouse and report. It is clear the werstings will not track that beast. Tell the Hikdar that I want an immediate check on all known menageries, zoos, arenas—we have to discover where that beast escaped from. And, by Vox, his owner will have a deal of explaining to do, believe me!"

"Quidang!"

"Tell all patrols to be on the alert—well, you don't need me to tell you your duty. Just look at this poor devil's throat. We have to find that animal, and fast."

Delia put a hand on my arm.

"I suppose you will go off—"

"Only until the prefect is alerted and we have men searching—"

"And I suppose Marion will wait?"

This was, indeed, a problem of etiquette.

As I pondered the implications, Seg broke in to say: "Did anyone recognize that beast? I did not."

"No—nor me." No one, it seemed, had any clear idea of just what kind of animal it was who had ripped out a poor fellow's throat.

A cloak was thrown over the corpse and the Watch lifted it up and prepared to carry it back to the guardhouse. The werstings were only too happy to leave.

I held Delia, and said, "Only as long as it takes, my heart. Marion will understand."

"Yes. She will."

"H'mm—that means she won't like it. Well, of course not. But by the same token that she does not want to start the evening until the emperor and empress arrive, I am the emperor and have my duties."

Seg said, "Milsi, my love, if you go with Delia Dray and I'll be along as soon as we can."

"Oh?" I said, as Milsi nodded immediate understanding acceptance.

"Too right, my old dom."

Sometimes there is no arguing with Seg Segutorio, with the wild mane of black hair and those fey blue eyes. If I was going off into what might appear a mundane business of reporting this killing and seeing that the hunt was up, he intended to be there too, just in case. . . .

With a beautifully controled touch of temper, Delia pointed out the obvious.

"The prefect will do all you can do, Dray."

"I expect nothing less. All the same—"

"Very well. Off you go. And don't be long!"

The mist swirled about us, clammy and concealing, as the ladies and their escorts reentered the narrow boat.

The smell of the water lifted to us, tangy and tinged with that strange scent of the canal waters of Vallia. Some of the Watch did not venture within six paces of the edge and were without the slightest interest in those slatey waters. Others walked near and did not mind. The first were not canalmen, and while the second might not be vens, either, they could drink of the water and not die.

The narrow boat vanished into the mist.

Seg and I and the others started off to the guardhouse.

"That monstrous brute worries me, Dray." Seg shook his head. "You know me, my old dom, and a hulking great monster scares me sometimes. But this one, this is different."

"We'll find out what idiot let him loose. You know the new laws prohibit wild-beast entertainments. Well, if I find some lout has been enjoying himself torturing animals and killing them in the name of sport—no wonder the thing attacked. It's probably hungry and thirsty, scared out of its wits, and ready to turn on anyone."

"True. And it's dangerous, Erthyr knows."

We did not spend long at the guardhouse. The Hikdar in command there jumped into action when we appeared. Mounted messengers were sent off galloping to warn the other precincts, search parties were organized, and a man was dispatched to haul the prefect out to take overall command. When all that was done Seg suggested we ought at last to take ourselves off to the party.

"Yes. And I own I am looking forward to it."

"I need a wet, and that is sooth."

"I'm with you there. Also, I'm interested in meeting this Strom Nango ham Hofnar."

Seg grimaced.

"The very sound of the name, here in Vondium, rings strange."

"Aye."

"Well, if Marion is set on marrying him, there's an end to it. These women, once they've made up their minds, are never deflected."

"You do not, of course, Seg, include the Lady Milsi in this wild and extravagant generalization?"

He had the grace to throw his handsome head back and roar with laughter.

"You may think you have me there, my old dom, but I tell you—I cannot say which one of us was the more eager."

The truth was, I was overjoyed that my blade comrade had at last found a lady. The Lady Milsi, who was Queen Mab of Croxdrin and who thusly had made Seg into King Mabo, I knew to be right for him, a wonderful lady, a great queen, and a girl any man would joy in. She'd had the sense to pick on Seg and go to very great lengths to make sure she won him. Very soon we would have to make arrangements to take her to the Sacred Pool of Baptism in the River Zelph in far Aphrasöe, the Swinging City. There the immersion in that magical milky fluid would confer on her not only a thousand years of life but the ability to throw off sickness and to recover from wounds in incredibly short times.

The narrow boat returned for us and we boarded

at the spot where this mysterious beast had killed his poor victim. We pushed off and floated near silently along the canal.

On duty tonight as escort were twelve men of the Second Regiment of the Emperor's Sword Watch. They made an interesting contrast among themselves. The 2ESW system provided training for young officers who would eventually go to places in the line as well as a corps of seasoned fighting men to take their place in the Guard Corps. So it was that among these twelve were to be found the hard-faced veterans of a hundred fights, and the beardless cheeks of lads just beginning their careers as soldiers.

Their crimson and yellow uniforms showed bravely in the lamplight, their weapons glittered brightly. The rest of the duty squadron would be waiting at Marion's villa where the party for her affianced groom was to be held.

As the craft glided along the canal I still felt a fretfulness at the back of my stupid old vosk skull of a head that by rights I ought to be out there in the streets and avenues of the city, a sword in my fist, leading the hunt for that monstrous and uncanny beast.

Echoing my thoughts, Seg grumped out: "Had I my bow with me . . ." He heaved up his shoulders, and finished: "I felt so confoundedly useless."

Lights bloomed ahead flooding down a warm yellow radiance. The mist wisped away. The narrow boat glided expertly into the space of water penned between two other boats and her way came off.

Nath Corvuus, the Jiktar in command of the duty squadron, tut-tutted and let out a: "By Vox! Someone will have a red face!"

Seg cocked an eye at me, and I own I smiled back.

The lads of the Guard Corps were mighty proud of their duties, and quick to resent any implied slight of the emperor or empress. It was clear that in Jiktar Nath's opinion, a space alongside the jetty should have been reserved for the emperor's boat and kept clear of all other craft. Well, this is all petty nonsense to me, but I had to maintain the gravitas and mien of your full-blooded emperor from time to time. Now was not the time.

"Let us not worry about that on a night like this, Nath. This is a pre-nuptial party. And remind your new lads again what will happen if they get drunk."

"Oh, aye, majister. I'll remind 'em."

Drunkenness, either on duty or off, was not a crime in the Vallian Imperial Guard Corps. The first offence would see the culprit run up in front of his Jiktar where he would be solemnly warned. The second offence was the last. The idiot would be discharged, not with ignominy, just sent off, and transferred to another unit of the line. There was much good-natured drinking in the Guard; there was practically never any drunkenness.

We hopped nimbly across the intervening boats and stepped onto the stone jetty. Here the duty squadron lined up, forming an alleyway bounded by crimson and yellow, by steel and bronze. The brave flutter of their feathers caught the torchlights. They were all at pike-stiff attention.

With that suitable gravitas Seg and I marched up between them to the porticoed entrance to Marion's villa. Here she stood forth to welcome us, as was proper. A crowd of guests clustered to one side. Delia and Milsi, looking absolutely marvelous, stood a little ahead of the rest. In the case of Delia, and Milsi, too, this was also perfectly proper. I am the last person in two worlds ever to forget that my gorgeous Delia, my Delia of Delphond, my Delia of the Blue Mountains, is an empress.

"Lahal, majister! Lahal and Lahal!"

"Lahal, my lady Marion. Lahal all."

The greetings were called, the people welcomed us, and very soon we were able to enter the villa and see about that wet.

But before that, the lady Marion came over and looking up said, "Majister. May I present Strom Nango ham Hofnar."

"Lahal, Strom, "I said, very formal, not smiling, but trying to be easy. "Lahal. You are very welcome to Vallia and to Vondium."

"Lahal, majister. I thank you. I bear a message from the emperor for you."

"Good! Nedfar and I are old comrades. I trust he is well and enjoying life to the full."

"Indeed yes, majister. To the full."

Studying this Nango ham Hofnar I was struck by his air of competence. He was not overly tall, yet he stood a head higher than the lady Marion. His hair, dark, was cut low over his forehead. There was about the squareness of his lips and jaw a reassurance. This man, I saw, was useful . . .

He wore gray trousers, a blue shirt and over his shoulders was slung a short bright green cape, heavily embellished with gold lace. This was smart evening wear in Hamal. Among the folk of Vallia he looked highly foreign and exotic.

Also, I noticed he wore a rapier and main gauche.

A great deal of the rigorous security maintained by my guards had been relaxed in recent seasons, and they now allowed people they didn't know to wear weapons in my presence, although they were still mighty jumpy about it, by Krun.

The Vallians here wore evening attire. Now your normal Vallian will wear soothing pastel colors in the evening, gowns most comfortable to lounge about in. This was a pre-nuptial party and the folk wore startling colors. This was all part of the fun and freedom of the occasion, of course. My Delia astounded me, at least, by wearing a brilliant scarlet robe, smothered in gold. This was a far cry from her usual laypom or lavender gown. Milsi's gown was a virulent orange. She and Delia had struck up a firm friendship, thank Zair, and Milsi was happy to be guided by the empress in matters of dress and protocol in this new land.

Yet, inevitably, there were very very few blue robes among that throng. Green, yes, Vallians have no objection to green. So, sizing up this Strom Nango, I guessed Marion had tactfully suggested he wear a differently colored shirt, and he'd simply smiled and said that he usually wore a blue one because it suited him.

After a few more words the strom was hauled off to meet other folk and Delia could corner me. We stood by a linen-draped table loaded with comestibles.

"Well? What happened?"

"Nothing. Seg and I just got things started and then left."

"I have not mentioned it here. Milsi and I thought it best. No need to spoil the party."

"Quite right."

"And your impressions of this Hamalese strom?"

"A tough character. Hidden depths. He's a pal of Nedfar's now, it seems, although he fought against us in the war."

Delia wrinkled up her nose. She knows full well how dangerous a thing for her to do in public that is. I managed to control myself.

"We beat the Hamalese in fair fight, the war is over, and now we're friends. You put Prince Nedfar on the throne of Hamal and made him emperor. And his son Tyfar and our daughter Lela are—"

"Zair knows where."

"So Marion presumably knows what she is doing."

I gave Delia a look I hoped was shrewd. "She is not a Sister of the Rose."

"Of the Sword."

"Ah."

"And we cannot stand talking together like this at Marion's party for her husband-to-be. It is not seemly. There is old Nath Twinglor who promised me a three-hundred-season-old copy of "The Canticles of the Nine Golden Heavens" and if his price is right I shall forgo a great deal of other fripperies. Now do you go and try to be pleasant to Sushi Vannerlan who is all by herself over there."

"Oh, no—" I began.

Very seriously, Delia said, "Sushi's husband, Ortyg, was recently killed. He fell in a battle Drak only narrowly won. It would be seemly."

Our eldest son Drak was still hammering away down there in the southwest of Vallia trying to regain the losses we had sustained when that rast of a fellow, Vodun Alloran, who had been the Kov of Kaldi, treacherously turned against us and proclaimed himself king of Southwest Vallia. As I walked slowly across to speak to Sushi Vannerlan, with the noise of the party in my ears and the scents of good food and wine coiling invitingly in the air, I reflected that I was not at all ashamed that I had not known Jiktar Ortyg Vannerlan had been slain in battle.

I'd been away in Pandahem until recently and was still in process of catching up with all that had gone on during my enforced absence.

Sushi was a slightly built woman, vivid and dark, and she'd painted on redness in lips and cheeks. Her eyes sparkled indicating the drops nestling there. Her dress was a shining carmine. Her hair fluffed a little, but it was threaded with gold and pearls. I feel I spoke the few necessary words with dignity and sincerity. Ortyg, her husband, had been a damned fine cavalry commander and I was sorry for all our sakes he was gone.

"Sushi!"

The voice, heavy and most masculine, sounded over my shoulder. Sushi jumped and genuine color flushed into her cheeks making the paint appear flaked and gaudy. She looked past me.

"Ortyg! Shush—this is the—"

"No matter who it is, they shall not steal you away from me!"

At the sound of the name Ortyg I felt for a moment, and I own it! that her husband had returned from the dead. Somehow this night with its mists and shifting moonlight had created an uneasy feeling in me. The swiftness and lethality of that shaggy beast seemed out of the world. And now Sushi was calling to her dead husband . . .

I turned sharply.

The man was like his voice, heavy and masculine. He wore the undress uniform of a cavalry regiment; he was a Hikdar, with two bobs, a bristly moustache, hard dark eyes, and a mouth full and ripe. His smile was a marvel.

"Ortyg! Please—"

"Now now, Sushi! I know I am late; but there had been a furor in the city and I was almost called out." He was not looking at me. "But my Jiktar let me off, may Vox shine his boots and spurs for evermore!"

As he spoke he advanced, still looking at Sushi, and made to pass me. I stood back. I was highly amused. Also, this tearaway cavalry man was doing all the right things for Sushi she needed and that I, despite being the emperor, could not do.

He put his left arm about her waist and then swung about, holding her, to face me. He was flushed and triumphant.

"I claim Sushi, my lad, and don't you forget it!"

Now I was wearing a rather stupid evening lounging robe of the self-same brilliant scarlet as that worn by Delia. This was her idea. So I looked a popinjay beside this cavalryman in his trim undress. The two bobs on his chest testified to two acts of gallantry in battle.

He saw me.

He didn't know who I was, that was clear, yet my face, despite that I was making heroic attempts to smile, caused him to flinch back.

"By Vox! Sushi—who—"

"I'm trying to tell you, you great fambly! Stand to attention, my dear." She looked at me, and she picked up her voice and it did not quiver, as she said:

"Majister, allow me to present to you Ortyg Voman, Hikdar in the Fifteenth Lancers. Ortyg, you stand in the presence of your emperor."

"Ouch!" said Hikdar Ortyg Voman, of the Fifteenth Lancers.

And I laughed.

Then I stuck out my hand. "Shake hands, Hikdar Ortyg. I know of the Fifteenth. Mind you take care of Sushi."

"Quidang, majister!"

Leaving these two to their cooing and billing I went off to see about a refill. The party really was a splendid affair. Marion, who was a stromni, had spared no expense. There must have been four or five hundred people circulating through the halls and galleries of her villa. Wine flowed in vast lakes and winefalls. Food weighed down the tables. Orchestras positioned at strategic points warbled tunes into the heated air without clashing one with the other.

Now Marion, the Stromni Marion Frastel of Huvadu, had quite clearly in my eyes not been able to pay for all this luxury herself. In these latter days Vondium and Vallia, it is true, had recovered considerably from the pitiless wars that had ravaged the country. We could throw a good shindig when we had to. But Marion's stromnate of Huvadu lay right up in the north, north of Hawkwa country in the northeast. It was barely south of Evir, the most northerly province of Vallia. All the land up there above the Mountains of the North was lost to we Vallians and was now ruled by some upstart calling himself the King of North Vallia. He raided constantly down into Hawkwa country, and we maintained a strong army up there to resist his encroaches.

This meant Marion's estates were lost to her, and therefore her wealth. It seemed to me that the Hamalese, Strom Nango, must have paid for this night's entertainment.

His stromnate, I gathered from Delia, lay in the Black Hills of Hamal, the most powerful empire in the continent of Havilfar south of the equator. He must either be wealthy himself or be spending lavishly now with an eye to the future. Marion's husband the late strom had only just inherited himself through a collateral relative. If Nango eventually lived up in Huvadu once we had regained the stromnate he'd find it damned cold after the warmth of Hamal.

If Marion decided to go to live in Hamal then she'd cope with the heat. She was a fine woman, not too tall, and full of figure, a strong and forceful personality who did not take kindly to fools. She had a way with her that could at times be misconstrued and sometimes turned people unable to see her good points against her. I wished her and this Nango well, and strolled off to catch a breath of air.

People nodded and smiled as I passed; but I did not stop to talk. A group of girls, laughing and clearly playing pranks on one another, rushed past. I raised my glass to them and they all replied most handsomely. They were all Jikai Vuvushis, I knew, Sisters of the Sword, most probably, in Marion's regiment. They fled off, shrieking with laughter, as far as one could imagine from the tough fighting women they were on the field of battle.

Out under a portico where the fuzzy pink light of the Maiden with the Many Smiles fell athwart the paving stones I spotted the serene face of Thantar the Harper. He was blind. He was not blind in the way that many a harpist was blinded on our Earth but as the result of an accident in youth. He wore a long yellow robe, and his acolyte walked a few paces astern carrying the harp. He would delight us later on in the evening with his songs and stories. He grasped a staff in his right hand and his left rested on the fair hair of a boy child who led him and was his eyes.

"Lahal, Thantar."

"Lahal, majister."

He knew my voice, then.

"I am most pleased to know you are here. You have a new song for us among all the old favorites?"

"As many as you please, majister." His voice rang like a gong, full and round. A splendid fellow, Thantar the Harper, renowned in Vondium.

A hubbub started beyond the edge of the terrace where the Moonblooms opened to the pink radiance and gave of their heady perfume. I looked across.

A group of roisterers with their backs turned to me staggered away to the sides. Their yells turned to screams. A man stepped through the gap between them, walking in from the terraced garden beyond. He carried a young lad in his arms.

The hard, tough, experienced face of Jiktar Nath Corvuus was crumpled in with grief and rage. No tears trickled down his leathery cheeks; but the brightness of his eyes, the flare of his nostrils, his ferociously protective attitude, told that he suffered.

In his arms he carried one of his young lads, the brilliant crimson and yellow uniform hideously bedraggled in blood and mud. The boy's helmet was lost and his brown hair shone in the lanternlight, swaying as Nath brought him in.

"Look!" choked out Nath Corvuus.

The boy's throat was a single red mass, a glistening bubble of horror.

CHAPTER TWO

THE GANCHARK OF THERMINSAX

We searched. Oh, yes, we searched.

Marion's villa yielded weapons enough to give us some confidence we might meet and face up to a gigantic beast. We shone lanternlight into the shrubberies and arcades, we thrashed the bushes. We shouted and banged kettles and pans.

We found not a sign of that feral horror.

The Watch of this precinct carried on the search farther into the streets and alleys. Seg and I felt firmly convinced the beast must be lurking low, sated by now on a victim he seized and killed without being disturbed.

"I don't want the whole city sent into a panic," I said to the prefect, who attended me at Marion's villa.

"Quite so, majister. We will prosecute the search with the utmost diligence; but I think we shall find nothing until the beast strikes again."

The prefect was a Pachak, Joldo Nat-Su, who had only two arms. He had been long employed by Naghan Vanki, the emperor's chief spymaster, and had lost his lower left in some fracas or other. Giving the post of city prefect in charge of the Watch to a man of Naghan Vanki's had seemed at the time sensible. He ran a tidy force and carried the honorary rank of Chuktar.

"I think you are right, Joldo, bad cess to it. Sink me!" I burst out. "We cannot have wild animals roaming the streets of Vondium! It is not to be borne!"

"If we are ready when it is seen," said Delia in her soothing and practical voice, "then we can catch it and cage it up again."

"Ah," said Prefect Joldo. "You say again, majestrix. So far my men have found no one who owns to having lost a caged animal."

"Too scared what'll happen to 'em," said Seg.

He held Milsi close and I fancied that no man or woman would willingly let their spouse out of their sight until this wild beast was safely caged—or killed.

Marion's party had incontinently wound up. Most of the guests had departed. There were just a few of us left, gathered in a small withdrawing room to talk over the events of the night.

Strom Nango kept to himself and made no effort to push forward or impose his views, and this pleased us. Everyone, including himself, realized he was on approval.

The Lord Farris leaned forward in his chair and said: "I'll put every soldier we have at your disposal, Joldo. I agree with the emperor. We cannot allow this kind of happening in the city."

Farris, the Kov of Vomansoir, was the emperor's justicar-crebent, or crebent-justicar, I could never worry over which way around the title went. He ran Vallia when Drak and I were away. He was a man with an intense loyalty to Delia, a man I trusted, the kind of man Vallia sorely needed.

The conversation became general then as we talked the thing inside out.

And, then, Thantar the Harper struck a chord and we all fell silent.

He sat sideways on his chair so that a samphron oil lamp's glow brought out the hollows of his blind eyes. His harp was quite small, resting between his knees, cunningly fashioned and probably two or three hundred years old. He used it to emphasize what he said, underlining the starker passages with grim chords, using ripples of sound to highlight a passage of action or love.

"You will delight us, Thantar?" said Delia. "We are in your debt that you accepted Stromni Marion's invitation. She is, I think, to be congratulated as well."

Marion looked pleased at this little piece of Delia's tomfoolery; but Delia was deadly serious about Thantar. Great artists are not bidden to perform in the politer courts of Kregen, whatever they get up to in the barbarian lands.

Thantar just said: "It is your presence, majestrix, that does us all the honor."

Well, so it was fulsome; he was dead right, too, by Vox!

In the rich and golden voice that appeared so incongruous issuing from so gaunt and desiccated a frame, Thantar began the story of The Ganchark of Therminsax.

Therminsax was the capital city of the Imperial province of Thermin, to the west of Hawkwa Country. From there a fine canal system extended southward. I recalled the iceboats that flew down from the Mountains of the North. Rough country around there, in places, and rich lands, too. With all the other romantic connections associated with Therminsax, I confess my own most important thought about the city was that it witnessed the creation of the Phalanx, the core of the army which had done so much to reunite and pacify Vallia.

Of course, by Zair, there was still a great deal to do. But then, that is the way of life. . . .

No one spoke as the blind harpist delivered his lines.

The story was of the olden time; but not too long ago, when savage beasts still roamed wild and free in many of the provinces of Vallia. The chark was one such wild animal, untamed, ferocious, cunning, pitiless in a special way that set it apart from your usual run of creatures of the wild. The charks normally hunted in packs and men said they possessed a primitive language of their own. Sometimes a single chark, either female or male, would go rogue, go lonely, wander off as a solitary. These became a menace to the surrounding territory. They were not to be classed, I understood as Thantar spoke on, with the man-eating tigers of India on our own Earth which are too old and slow to catch much other game than humans.

These solitary charks were among the most powerful of the packs.

As he described the beast in glowing words, the Kregish rolling and fierce, subtle and cunningly hinting, I saw in my mind's eye a picture of the beast I had seen on the towpath. That had been a chark. I felt sure of it.

Charks, said Thantar, were considered to be extinct. None had been reliably reported in Vallia for many years, although some men boasted they had seen the gray shaggy forms slinking through the back hills of Hawkwa country.

Then a rash of bloodthirsty killings set all Therminsax on edge. No one was safe. A mother taking her child to school wearing her best dress was set on and slain. Blood splashed the pretty dress, and the hunters followed the trail until they came upon the grisly remains. Men out in the woods burning charcoal were ripped to shreds. The city itself was not safe, for the great beast seemed able to steal in as and when he pleased, to take a life in blood-welling horror.

Traps were set. All were unsuccessful.

Listening intently, I admired the masterful way in which Thantar included blood and death and horror in describing each incident, and yet did not overburden his narrative with so much blood and death and horror as to offend the susceptibilities of the ordinary person. Only the ghoulish and perverted would complain at the lack. Only the sadist would demand more agony.

A change overtook the story. Now Thantar spoke with hindsight, telling us things that were afterwards discovered and deduced, facts unknown at the time of the events.

Even with all the hindsight, the wise men had been unable to tell how the young man, Rodo Thangkar, had first become a werewolf.

He had been a happy, carefree young fellow, training to be a stylor, reasonably well-connected. He had hoped to marry his childhood sweetheart, Losha of the Curled Braids. She was one of the earliest victims of the terror, her face slashed to ribbons, her throat torn out by the fangs of the werewolf.

As the City Elders discussed what to do, and set their traps, young Rodo Thangkar stood by, learning his trade as a stylor and under his master's tuition taking down notes of all that was said and decided.

No wonder the werewolf evaded all the traps with such contemptuous ease!

The reign of terror continued and the ganchark continued to exact a hideous toll of the folk of Therminsax and the surrounding countryside.

Many brave fighting men, champions, came to the city to strike blows with their swords and spears against the ganchark. None survived. Their mangled bodies were reverently buried, and the folk sighed, and stayed close to home.

The City Elders pleaded with anyone to come and help them in their time of trial. Sorcerers and wizards did, indeed, journey to Therminsax. One of them, A Sorcerer of the Cult of Almuensis, boasted that no ganchark could stand against the awful powers locked in his great book chained to his waist.

He was a glittering figure in his robes and jewels, girded with gold, the hyrlif itself a book exuding the aura of thaumaturgy. They found him with his head detached from his body, lying in the roadside ditch. His forefinger was still in place in the half-opened book. It was clear to all that the werewolf had leaped long before the sorcerer had had time to read out the curse to free the land of this terror.

From his island came Goordor the Murvish, of the Brotherhood of the Sorcerers of Murcroinim. He stank. He wore wild animal pelts, belts of skulls, and carried a montarch, the heavy staff crowned with rast skulls and dangling with objectionable portions of decayed organic matter. Yet he wore swords.

He said he would relieve the city of Therminsax of its werewolf for one thousand gold talens.

The City Fathers collected the money in a single hour.

So young Rodo Thangkar listened to this transaction,

and he smiled, and perhaps he raised a hand to his mouth to polish up a tooth.

He, himself, said the story, could not explain why he did what he did, why he transformed himself into a werewolf.

The following night when all the good folk of the city lay fast, the confrontation took place. No man or woman witnessed that sight. Nothing was heard.

In the morning they were found, the sorcerer and the young man, lying near to each other. The ganchark had resumed his form as a man in the moment of death, the sorcerer's dudinter sword through him. And the sorcerer lay crumpled with no face, no throat, no breast. Blood spattered everywhere.

Thantar the Harper finished with a thrumming chord, and said: "So Therminsax was rid of the evil, and the thousand gold talens were never given to the sorcerer Goordor the Murvish but were used to provide a great feast in thanksgiving."

When the last vibrating note dwindled to silence no one spoke, no one stirred. There was no applause. We all sat like dummies, the words spinning in our heads.

Then, bursting out like a thunderclap, the Lord Farris snapped: "No! Impossible. I do not believe it!"

Strom Nango began: "The story, or the——?"

"The story is a story, well calculated to frighten children, and exciting too, I daresay. But as for the conclusion you all seem to wish to draw—no!"

"Tsleetha-tsleethi," said Seg. "Softly-softly. These tales are known. Werewolves are known also."

Delia remained silent.

Milsi looked troubled, and I noticed the way she gripped Seg's hand, her nails biting into his palm.

Marion said: "I'm not sure. Oh, I used to love all

these ghostie and ghoulie stories when I was young. They have a treasury of them in the north—but, this—it is so horrible—can one believe? Is it possible? A werewolf at large, here in Vondium?"

Various of the other people in this small select gathering expressed similar views. How could a legend of the past spring into vivid life in this day and age?

Thantar the Harper, having sowed this seed, remained silent. One could not help wondering what was going on in his mind. He had told this story with meaning, with a purpose. A blind man, could he see more than we sighted ones?

Strom Nango bent and whispered in Marion's ear.

She turned her head up, smiling at him, and I saw there was love there.

"You are right, my dear." She turned to face us, and prefacing her remarks with flattering references to the emperor and empress in our midst, she said: "This is too gloomy and horrendous a subject. My party for dear Nango I will not have completely ruined. He has suggested we move on to more salubrious subjects—"

"Oh, indeed, yes!" exclaimed Milsi.

"Very well." Here Marion glowed with inner pleasure. "Thantar and I have devised a new story, one that is supremely worth the telling. I hope, soon, that Thantar will set it to suitable music. But, at the moment . . ."

"At the moment," rang the golden voice of the harpist, "the story is worthy in its own right, a story of high courage and selfless devotion."

We all called out, demanding that Thantar delight us with this new and wonderful story.

CHAPTER THREE

OF A HILLSIDE IN HAMAL

Among the harsh rocks of the Hamalian Mountains of the West a small party of warriors huddled behind boulders or in scrapes painfully dug from the barren and stony soil. There were perhaps twenty of them, twenty soldiers left from the eighty that had formed their pastang. They were tired, thirsty, hungry, blood-shot of eye, striped with wounds, and each one knew that the end could not be far off.

Penning them in, ringing them in a hoop of steel, a horde of the wildmen from the vasty unknown lands beyond the mountains were content for the moment to shoot into the pitiful stronghold, to rush closer in a swirl of noise and action to draw return shots, to drop down—and to wait. Soon the soldiers would have no more shafts to stem the final attack.

This scene, painful though it was, held no originality.

So long as the civilized lands patrolled the borders and contested the notion that the wildmen might raid with impunity, then just so long would parties be cut off and surrounded and exterminated. This was the savage and pitiless species of warfare prac-ticed along the Mountains of the West now that the Empire of Hamal had retracted from its westward march of triumph.

There was no question that the bloodthirsty moor-krim from the wild lands of the west could over-whelm and destroy these last few soldiers. But the wildmen taunted their victims, showed themselves to draw a shaft, and dropped flat again. They did not pour in in a last lethal tide of death. No doubt the chief concern in the primevally savage and cunning head of the moorkrim chieftain was that the trapped soldiers would all commit suicide before his men could lay hands on them.

For the soldiers forming the remnant of the pastang trapped on that desolate hillside were Jikai Vuvushis, Warrior Maidens, every one.

Some distance to the east in the foothills of the ragged mountain chain stood the tumbledown fron-tier town of Hygonsax. Dust lay thickly everywhere, the suns scorched, hardy semi-desert vegetation drooped in the heat. The adobe fort from which floated the flags of two regiments appeared sunk in lethargy.

One flag displayed the number and devices of the One Hundred Twenty-Sixth Regiment of Aerial Cavalry of Hamal. The other, less obvious, more cryptic, told those who understood that this standard was of the Seventh Regiment, SOS, of Vallia.

Both treshes hung limply against the flagstaffs.

The only sounds were of a calsany moodily kicking a mudbrick wall, and the scrape, scrape, scrape of a little gyp scratching himself for fleas.

In a sudden rush of leathery wings, an aerial patrol whistled over the town. The mirvols extended their claws to seize the perching poles and folded their wings. The riders, stiffly, walking like men who have been too long aloft in the saddle, moved thankfully to their quarters where they might try to wash away the dust inside and out. Their commander fairly ran into the fort and through to the wide, cool room past an abruptly galvanized sentry.

The woman striding uncertainly about the commander's room turned expectantly.

"You have found them?"

Jiktar Nango ham Hofnar halted, embarrassed at his news, depressed, cross, feeling the heat and the strain as though an iron helmet crushed down about his brows.

"I am sorry, Jiktar Marion."

"Then it must be all over with them—"

"I cannot believe that."

"But you have searched everywhere. Your patrols have flown day and night. How could they still be alive without your finding them?"

"I do not know, but I do know that I shall not rest until we have found the answer, one way or another."

Jiktar Nango swayed as he spoke, and put a quick hand to the back of a chair. He gripped the wood harshly, supporting himself.

Instantly, Marion darted forward. She took his arm and made him sit down, and then fetched a pitcher and glass. She poured parclear, and the bright fizzy drink sparkled in the mingled radiance of the suns falling between the columns of the adobe house's open walls. She looked at him critically, and frowned.

"You have not slept for three days and nights. You cannot go on like this, Jikar Nango."

"I must. You know that."

"But my girls—"

"Your girls are my responsibility out here. I marched with King Telmont against your emperor, and then with him we fought the damned Shanks at the Battle of the Incendiary Vosks. I hated all Vallians. But now—" He drank again, feeling the fizzy liquid cleaving a path down his throat, tingling his toes. "Now we are allies. I shall not rest, Jikar Marion, never, until we know!"

She understood enough to know that this man spoke with honest conviction. He had hated Vallians; now he was allied to them. But it was not just that causing him to labor so strenuously. He was concerned for her Warrior Maidens, anxious for them, feeling this a matter of honor. He was a man of high chivalry determined to do all and more that could be done. If he killed himself doing it, he'd have only mundane regrets, none for the style of the thing.

Nango lay back in the chair and his eyelids drooped. Watching him, Marion felt an emotion to which she could not, she would not, put a name.

He jerked as a tremor contracted his muscles and then, like a man breasting a swift and treacherous current, he opened his eyes and struggled up onto his feet.

"What am I thinking of!" His left hand raked down to his sword hilt and gripped. "By Krun! Those rascals of mine had better be ready."

"But you've only just returned—"

"The mirvols brought us back. They are exhausted. And I expected good news . . ."

He glanced at the sand clock on its shelf and made a face. "I gave instructions the patrol could wash, eat and drink and be out on parade again in a single bur. We have enough mirvols to provide second string mounts for us all. So, I must bratch."

Bratching, as Marion could see, meant in Jiktar Nango's book jumping very hard and very fast indeed.

Heavy-winged, the mirvols took off in scurries and flurries of dust. The yellow drifted in the air, and settled, and added another fine coating to roofs and walls. She watched the flying animals wing away aloft, shading her eyes against the bright dazzlement of Zim and Genodras, which here in Havilfar are called Far and Havil, and the sensation of helplessness made her dizzy, so sick and powerful it fell upon her.

In order to retain any semblance of normality she had to convince herself that the pastang lost in the hills was not destroyed. The girls had had food and water for a number of days, plenty of shafts, a local guide, and unbounded confidence. The Seventh Regiment, SOS, had recently been assigned this duty out here along the Mountains of the West. Vallia and Hamal, allied, shared a common interest in preventing the raiding incursions of the wildmen, for the moorkrim had recently destroyed one of the famous flying islands. That had seen the loss of much-needed production for the airboats' silver boxes that lifted and propelled them through thin air.

The scattered detachments of the regiments were being called in. But, right here and now, Nango and she had only their small patrols to call on to prosecute the search.

Even when Nango returned, more haggard, more exhausted, she still clung doggedly to her belief that although it seemed inevitable that it must be all over for her girls, Nango's persistence must find them in the end.

"I shall fly with you, Nango—"

"But—!"

"I shall."

"Very well."

He gave instructions that flying leathers should be found for the Jiktar Marion, and a good strong clerketer. He inspected this harness personally. With this an aerial rider was fastened to the saddle; if it broke in the air—splat!

"I have the strongest conviction, Marion, it is strange, very strange. I know—it is in my bones, my blood—that we shall find your girls. And, even stranger, I know we shall find them alive. Not all, perhaps, but there have been odd portents reported—"

"Surely you don't believe mumbojumbo!"

"No. Nothing like two-headed ordels, or Havil drenched in the blood of Far. It is in me. We fly in half a bur, Marion. Are you ready?"

His change of tone jolted her. She nodded. "I am ready, Nango."

How Nango mounted his flying animal, how he had the strength to buckle himself in, grasp the reins, how he summoned the dregs of energy to kick in his heels, all astounded Marion. By Vox! She was tired. But Nango had flown continuously since the pastang had not reported in when it should have, and although his men had flown by rotation, Nango had flown on every patrol.

The man was clearly past the end of his resources; yet his sense of honor, his desire to uphold his own esteem of his regiment and his nation, drove him on.

Also, suspecting her own feelings, Marion guessed there were other similar forces at work in this Hamalese.

The leathery wings of the mirvols beat heavily against the warm air. They flew low over the rounded hills, cutting corners, edging higher into the jagged valley gashes between peaks. Everywhere the contused landscape of desolation met the eye.

Gripping on tightly, feeling the rush of wind blustering past, swaying with the floating, soaring and sinking sensations of the flying animal, Marion found she could cope perfectly well with flying. Given time, she might quite come to like it. She narrowed her gaze against the windrush and peered ahead.

The patrol skirted a jagged cliff edge where a few small birds of prey were quite content to let these large flyers sail past. Flying beasts of that size would find nothing to live on here, where the prey consisted of insects, lizards, animals constituted to live on practically nothing. Around that edge the valley opened out, peaks on either hand lofting against the dazzlement. Ahead of the patrol the eroded valley dozed in the heat.

The four-man advance echelon wheeled up into the sky, and one came hammering back.

He handled his mirvol with consummate, unthinking skill, swirling to fly wing-beat to wing-beat with Nango.

"Jiktar! Many dead bodies ahead!"

Marion's heart went thump in her breast.

Nango thwacked his beast and the flyer surged ahead. Marion copied him and only the leather straps of the clerketer saved her from falling back over the animal's tail.

In a vast swishing of wings the mirvols circled the site of the tragedy.

There were many dead bodies. Many of them. The moorkrim littered the stony ground. They lay abandoned in the attitudes of death, ringing the central area where a semblance of a fortress had been constructed from sangars and scrapes.

Within that central space lay the girls of the Seventh Regiment of the Sisters of the Sword.

As Marion gazed down, the whole scene wavered in the heat waves, and she could feel the blood bursting in her head, the fiery sting behind her eyes, the sense of desolation and panic and misery—and anger.

A tanned arm lifted. A brown-haired head turned to look up. Another arm waved.

Marion swallowed.

Nango shouted: "They live!"

Somehow, in an uproar of wings and fountains of dust, the patrol was down, landing in any cleared space among the bodies. Marion's fingers wrestled with the stubborn buckle of the harness, and the fool thing would not come undone, and Nango was there, his hard tired face smiling, to free the buckle and assist her to alight. They ran across to the nearest sangar, stumbling in among the piled boulders, ignoring the sprawled wreckage of the wildmen on the way.

It was all a wonder and a salvation.

Hikdar Noni Thostan managed to stand up and salute as her regimental commander ran up. She was dirty, disheveled, wounded, her uniform and armor tattered and dangling; yet she smiled as Jiktar Marion approached.

"Noni—Thank Opaz!"

"Marion—Thank Opaz you came . . . I've lost good girls—too many—they are gone—"

There were nineteen living survivors and one about to die.

Nango saw to everything that had to be done, moving with quickness, speaking with authority, and his men jumped to obey. The shambles was clear and hideous. The girls had fought a good fight. Yet . . .

Arrangements were put in hand to transport the living and the dead back to Hygonsax. The Hamalese swods, simple fighting men of the air, spoke in low tones. Nango kept himself on his feet and moving only by a final effort of willpower. He did say: "I could swear we flew up this valley two days ago." But his mind worked sluggishly now. When he had slept and refreshed himself would be the time to rejoice at this marvelous deliverance.

The moorkrim were left where they lay. Their flying saddle animals, tyryvols mostly, had all flown off long since. Marion bent to study one dead wildman. She shuddered. The viciousness in those harsh browned features, the tribal markings, the decorations, all spoke eloquently of a life far removed from that of civilization.

The man bore no mark of wounds; yet he was dead and all his viciousness would slough and decompose as the body rotted and he joined the food chain of the mountains.

The elation that nineteen of her girls had survived could not alter the sorrow that the rest of the pastang had died. So many fine young girls from Vallia, trained up by the Sisters of the Sword, smart and skilled, courageous, eager, and now all lying dead in their neat rows and ready for burial. Marion went through the funeral ceremony numbly.

She could taste the ceremonial wine they had drunk before the regiment left Vallia, still see in the eye of memory the long refectory tables, the candles, smell the flowers so tenderly cared for. As though less than a single heartbeat separated that farewell dinner, she was here, in Hamal, among the dust and heat and flies, the smells of so different a nature. The effort of opening her eyes to look at Nango as he spoke the words he felt necessary consumed her.

Her own emotions were forcing her on, and she could foresee in part what the future might hold.

Less than a heartbeat . . .

The regiment had marched out with the bands and the banners. Duty called them to a hard life here in the Mountains of the West of Hamal. She had met this hard, competent Jiktar of Aerial Cavalry, this Strom Nango ham Hofnar. It seemed to her less than a heartbeat ago she had left Vallia to serve overseas, and now here she was overseas and in Hamal and far too many of her fine young girls were dead . . .

Such misery she did not think she could bear alone. As the ceremony concluded with the proprieties reverently fulfilled, and she walked slowly away, she looked across at Nango. At the same moment he turned to look at her.

In that moment, in the enervating heat and the dust tasting of schoolroom chalk in her mouth, her gaze met Nango's. Oblivious of heat, of dust, of flies, negating everything else, they stared one at the other, and their futures were settled.

CHAPTER FOUR

WE DISAGREE OVER THE WEREWOLF OF VONDIUM

Delia hurled her slipper at me. Catching the silky scrap in my left hand I instantly hurled it back. She ducked, laughing at me, whipped off the other slipper and chucked that one at my head. When I raked out a hand to grab it she leaped the bed and was on me, bearing me down, ramming my back hard into the rug.

"D'you cry quarter, you fambly? Do you bare the throat?"

"Aye, aye, my love, I bare the throat. And my back's digging in most uncomfortably."

She kissed me lightly and then let me up. I wriggled around and sat up and put an exploratory hand down.

"More like digging into *you!*" she said, and laughed. I hauled out the big black riding boot and did not throw it at her. She sat up, flushed, radiant, divine. Well, there are no words too great or grand or divine in themselves for Delia of the Blue Mountains.

"What irks you, then, my heart?" I spoke philosophically, starting to rummage around for my clothes. The hour was still early, but we had a lot to do today.

"I am trying to prevent myself from feeling amusement instead of annoyance that Marion's party was spoiled—well—" Here she reached for the laypom-colored slip trailed across the bed-end, "well, not exactly spoiled. But the werewolf story, and that poor guard of yours, and the rest of it. I do not think Thantar the Harper's great new story about Marion and Nango was as well received as it otherwise would have been."

"Amusement?"

"You know what I mean. Anyway, I am positive I am preventing that feeling. Marion is a dear. And she has ambitions. She—"

"She is, of course, of the Sisters of the Sword and not of the Sisters of the Rose."

"The SOS put more regiments of Jikai Vuvushis into the field than the SOR. But they do not use the Claw or the Whip, as we do. Now I am not going to talk any more about that. I think I will pay her a call today. That will please her. And her Nango looks—h'mm? useful?"

"A sound fellow."

"So I deemed him."

"Although, mind you, I own I was a little disappointed in Thantar's story. I have told you of the time Jaezila—"

She interrupted not sharply but firmly.

"Yes, my dear. I still think of our daughter Lela as Lela, and not as Jaezila. I am sure you think of her as Jaezila."

"Yes."

Well, there was no mystery in that. After all, I'd adventured and fought with Jaezila long before I knew she was my daughter Lela. I went on:

"That time Jaezila and Seg and me went off to rescue Prince Tyfar and his father from the wildmen in the Mountains of the West—it must have been a very similar scene."

Delia has had to suffer greatly in her life since she first met me. I own I ache for her, and feel guilt and remorse. But, she is a princess, an empress, and hollow though the titles may be to some, she is a very great lady. She is, also, cunning, shrewd, subtle, tough and altogether enchanting—and damned infuriating. She had come to terms with her extraordinary life long before I'd told her I'd never been born on Kregen; but came from a small planet orbiting a yellow sun that was, by the standards of Zim and Genodras, very small and insignificant. And it had only one silver moon, to boot, and possessed no splendid array of human beings not built in the same mold as apims, as Homo sapiens sapiens, like Delia and me.

"We saw the wildmen off that time, thanks to a very brave Hamalese officer and his men. But, all the same, I own I was a trifle disappointed with the story—"

"We were all tired by then. And the werewolf did not help—"

"You mean the story of the werewolf?"

"Yes."

The breeches I pulled on were sober Vallian buff. The tunic on its stand was of buff. This day I was to begin by officiating at the opening ceremony for a whole new complex of houses and shops. Slowly we were rebuilding Vondium, trying to make the once proud city vital and alive again.

"The story of the werewolf did not cheer us up, true. All the same," and here I tightened up the lesten-hide belt and rummaged around for the boots that had so sorely assaulted me. I felt—to use the imagery of another age—that the snapper was lacking in Thantar's story of Marion and Nango. There was no punchline. I said as much to Delia as I buttoned up the tunic.

"You could say, could you not, my dyspeptic Dray, that the fact we heard the story at all was its suitable finale. Marion and Nango are happy. Surely, one might think, that is a quittable ending?"

I eyed her cautiously.

"One might."

Delia's first task this day was to open a new hospital and rest home for invalid soldiers. The usual customs of earlier times on our own Earth and to a great degree on Kregen, of employing soldiers when needed and when the war was over of discharging them to starve and die in the gutter, could not be allowed to continue in the new Vallia we were building.

The problems did not arise where mercenaries were hired. This had been one of the sticks my opponents had beaten me with when we'd been creating a true Army of Vallia to replace the mercenary forces heretofore used. My reasons for the decision were plain and commonsense. Now we had to pay the reckoning.

Delia instead of drawing on tall black riding boots put on softer, lower boots. For the proper atmosphere to be created when she attended the hospital opening she would ride in her palanquin. The gherimcal, carried by her corps of Womoxes, would give just that necessary extra feeling of the presence of the empress without the harsh reminder that trampling hooves would have brought. At least, that was the theory . . .

"With you, Dray Prescot," she said with some considerable mock-tartness, "one might anything!"

"True, true—and I still think the story lacking."

"Maybe Thantar should have ended it earlier, at the moment of rescue."

"Marion wanted to show the results. The girls have been brought home, and she is on a furlough, although—"

"That, my dear, will be the business of the Sisters of the Sword."

My early feelings of abhorrence that women should fight as soldiers, bequeathed to me from my upbringing on Earth at the end of the eighteenth century, persisted only in certain cases here on Kregen. Folk regarded me as a loon when I stumblingly tried to explain my reactions. If women demand equality with men in all things, as well as their already achieved superiority in others, then they can damn well shoulder a weapon and go off and fight. That was *that* theory . . .

So when in some mysterious way I found that I was to have another bodyguard force to add to those already created, the fact that this corps was to be composed of Jikai Vuvushis did not discompose me as it would have done before. It seemed that all the women were agreed. If the Empress Delia could have regiments of men in her bodyguard, then the emperor could have a regiment of women—surely?

Two splendid numim girls, lion-maidens, Mich and Wendy, had taken the initial steps—when my back was turned, I might add—and an emperor's regiment of Jikai Vuvushis was recruiting.

With that eerie but wonderfully warming meeting of thoughts, Delia effortlessly picked up on the subject in my mind from what she had been saying.

"Marion's duties, as you must guess, concern your new guard regiment. How much she wishes to tell you about the SOS must remain for her to decide."

"If she tells me twice as much as you tell me about the Sisters of the Rose, that will still be nothing."

"Which is as it must be," said Delia, primly infuriating.

Just as we were leaving the bedchamber to go down to the first breakfast, Delia put her hand on my shoulder.

"Dray—suppose there is a werewolf running loose in Vondium?"

Her tone pushed aside any inane reply of denying the possibility. Delia was penetrating through to the eventuality that a ganchark might really exist, and if so, what were we to do about it. On Kregen they do not take so lightly the stories of the undead, the kaotim, stories of lycanthropy, as we do on Earth. Delia was being highly practical. If a ganchark intended to terrorize Vondium, we ought at least to have thought seriously about the problem and the measures we could take in self-defense.

My reply was therefore considered.

"We must summon all the sorcerers and wizards who may give us answers. Thantar's story suggested there is an answer. We must find, if it is necessary, the appropriate answer now."

"Yes. I do not wish to think of it; but if it is necessary then we must."

"After you have seen to your hospital and I to my complex, we must meet with Nath na Kochwold. He is clamorous regarding the Fifth Phalanx—"

"You worry too much, my dear. The Phalanxes have proved their worth in battle—"

"Surely. They triumph. But I do still worry over the numbers of men tied up in the brumbyte files."

We had four Phalanxes with a fifth building. One

was up in the northeast, one was with Turko in the midlands, one and a half were with Drak in the southwest. So we needed a fifth. Yet for every soldier trailing his pike as a brumbyte in the phalanx files, we might have trained up an archer, a kreutzin, a churgur. Oh, yes, it takes a special kind of fellow to be a brumbyte and maneuver pike and shield close packed with his comrades, but, all the same . . .

Going into the first breakfast we were met with luscious odors and the incessant rattle of animated conversation. Most folk of Kregen like to sit down for one of the breakfasts, usually the first, and then take the second standing up, filled with the doings of the morning and aware of what remains to be done before the hour of mid.

More often than not I took both breakfasts—when I was fortunate enough to eat two—standing up.

The room lay awash in the early rays of the twin suns. Folk were eating and chattering away nineteen to the dozen. Schemes were hatched, plans laid, news reported at this time. Helping Delia and myself to a considerable quantity of breakfast we went over to a group centered on Farris, who looked as calm, competent and in complete command as he always did.

The subject of conversation was, inevitably, the werewolf of Vondium.

Perforce I had to let the talk run on. Any attempt to block off speculation would only arouse more. Balancing a plate and a cup and eating is all very well for folk with three or four arms, or a tail hand, for apims like me with only two hands the process is highly demanding. I listened, chewing, weighing up what was said and what were different people's reactions.

Some just poo-poohed the whole idea.

Others would believe if there was sufficient proof.

A goodly number were perfectly convinced that a werewolf was running loose in the streets of the capital.

Pallan Myer, stooped over as ever from hours of reading, coughed his dry little tickler of a cough. He was the Pallan of Learning, responsible for education, and now he gave evidence of the way he regarded these stories.

"Utter balderdash. Quite unconvincing. The smallest child in my schools would laugh at this nonsense, for it defies credibility by its lack of logic."

"But logic," pointed out Nath na Kochwold, "is not necessary when one is dealing with the supernatural."

One or two interrupted at this; but Nath went on: "At least, not logic as it is understood by pedants. Internal logic, of course, is essential, otherwise the world would come to an end. We need far more evidence yet before any sound judgments may be made."

"I agree," said Farris, and put a paline into his mouth and chewed. For many people there that was the end of the argument.

One of these fine days, when Nath na Kochwold could be weaned away from his only true love—the Phalanx—he might well find himself standing where Farris now stood.

"My father," he said, "is Nazab Nalgre na Therminsax, who is the emperor's justicar governing all the province of Thermin. In Thermin you will find many folk who devoutly believe in the existence of gancharks."

Senator Naghan Strander, a member of the Presidio, glanced across at the Lord Farris before replying, as though to say that Farris had ended the conversation but there was just this little codicil.

"If the proof is forthcoming we must be prepared to meet it."

Delia looked at me and I knew what she was thinking. By meeting the proof, Naghan Strander openly accepted that that proof would be positive, that werewolves did exist and that one was terrorizing Vondium.

CHAPTER FIVE

CONCERNING THE PHALANX

The day passed, as days do pass with work accomplished but not enough—by Zair! never enough—to make me feel I'd earned my daily crust.

Truth to tell, with the Lord Farris and the Presidio we had set up perfectly capable of dealing with the problems of empire and the woes of Vallia, there was for me really only left the showy, emperor-type of function. Farris ran the place when I was not here, for which I gave thanks to Opaz, and I had no intention of making any attempt to usurp his functions.

When Drak at last threw out Vodun Alloran from the southwest and returned to Vondium in triumph, then Farris would gracefully retire from his position as Justicar Crebent and let Drak get on with it. Farris's heart was with the Vallian Air Service.

So it was that I opened the complex of houses and shops, then, after the second breakfast, went on to officiate at other functions. Much of Vondium at this time still lay in ruins. We concentrated on rebuilding the most essential structures first. When it was time to see Nath na Kochwold about his new Fifth Phalanx I brightened considerably.

With those thoughts occasioned by the kind of day I'd had I said to Nath as we stood in the anteroom leading from the barracks out to the square: "Well, Nath, there is only so much money and only so many resources. If we spend a thousand gold pieces to build a new school and what-have-you, there are a thousand talens less topside to pay the army and equip the lads."

"A school will not stop those rasts who raid us."

I pulled my ear. "Yet it may teach the youngsters what they will need to know for our future."

"They need to know how to shoulder a pike, to handle a shield, to wield a sword."

"Inter alia, inter alia."

Using the Kregish, the meaning was plain, and Nath smiled.

"You are, of course, majis, quite right. But, all the same—"

"All the same, my fiery kampeon, somehow we will build the schools and hospitals and find the wherewithal to fund the troops—even if the brumbytes in the files, being good soldiers, wear the old vosk-skull helmets still."

Seg walked in at that point and, overhearing, laughed.

"Vosks have skulls as thick through as Mount Hlabro. And, you know what has been said about our skulls."

"Aye," I said. Many and many a time I'd been told I had a skull as thick as a vosk's. Being an emperor made no difference there . . .

"Now, Nath," said Seg, very briskly. "I do not pretend to the pikes in the Phalanx. I've come to see about you archers. Dustrectium* is, after all, the secret of success."

---

* Dustrectium. Firepower as applied to the effects from archery, slings and engines.

—A.B.A.

"They come along, Seg," said Nath. "They come along. But, of course, they will never satisfy your standards."

He spoke only half mockingly.

Seg nodded, still sharp.

"True. But we must do what we can."

Trumpets pealed outside.

"Time to go."

So, out we went, all dressed resplendently for the occasion, and saw the Fifth Phalanx go through its paces.

"Commendable," I s'id. I did not commit myself further.

Seg puffed a little air between pursed lips, and said nothing.

The Fifth Phalanx contained the Ninth and Tenth Kerchuris, each totaling 5,184 brumbytes, 864 Hakkodin and a chodku of 864 archers.

"The ranks are well-filled," observed Seg.

"Aye." Here Nath stuck a fist onto his sword hilt and stared at Seg. "We had to use the old Fifth Phalanx to replace men leaving. The Tenth Kerchuri— the old Tenth—fought brilliantly at the Battle of Ovalia. The Ninth had a bad time down in the southwest, along with the Eighth from the Fourth Phalanx, when that cramph Vodun Alloran betrayed his trust and traitorously turned against us."

"I heard."

"There are enough men in this new Tenth to warrant the battle standards, and the honors. I have attempted to build a tradition into the phalanx force."

"And you have succeeded, Nath," I said, speaking with some force.

"I think, if you will permit, Nath," and Seg spoke

seriously, "I would like to spend a little time with your chodku. The bowmen can be smartened up."

We knew Seg was not speaking of drill or uniform but of the controlled discharges of flights of arrows, of the rhythm and speed. Seg Segutorio is the finest bowman of two worlds, for my money, and he would work wonders with these lads, even though they were not Bowmen of Loh.

"You will have my gratitude, Seg."

As the Phalanx, neatly divided into its various component parts, marched, my attention left Nath and Seg discussing just what Seg would do. Well, and, of course, the Phalanx looked superb! The lads could, at least, march in rank and file and keep their pikes all aligned. The red flags flew. The uniforms, plain and sensible with much hard leather and bronze, gave plenty of room for strenuous activity. The shields—what the swods in the ranks call the crimson flowers, among other less flattering names—all at the same angle, just then caught gleams of light from the two suns and all together flashed in combined reflections like a bolt of lightning.

I make no apology for mentioning the Phalanx. To have lived and to have seen the Phalanx in motion is to have lived twice over. Yes, the brumbytes in their files were superb. And, staring out with my emotions all stirred higgledy-piggledy by the realities of comradeship and war and peace and repugnance I have often spoken of, I refused to be struck by a self-indulgent and maudlin thought—"What is all this for?"

At my back the duty squadron of 2ESW sat their zorcas in what of patience they could summon. This was not the same squadron as the one on duty yesterday. I had an unpleasant task before me there, for the young lad whose throat had been torn out, Jurukker Larghos Vontner, had a father and mother and they had been informed and an appointment arranged at the earliest possible moment.

They would be traveling up from their small estate in the country now, shattered by this evil news.

This black thought made me turn my head away from the glittering and gorgeous pageant of the Phalanx to stare balefully at the duty squadron. They, of course, looked the splendid bunch of rapscallions they were, hardened old kampeons and fuzz-faced youngsters. I sighed.

Then I stared harder.

By Vox!

Along at the end of the line, tagged on, a group of zorcariders sat as silently and as still as the rest of the juruk. These riders did not have fuzz-faces. Their faces were smooth. Their eyes in the shadow of each helmet sometimes flashed a liquid gleam; their armor was of a different shape. I looked at them, these Jikai Vuvushis, and I realized that so far I'd been lucky—supremely fortunate—not to have to worry my head personally over the fate of a bunch of hare-brained girls in the day-to-day problems of running an empire. Now, if assassins struck, I'd be more concerned over these warrior ladies—

I halted my runaway thoughts.

Idiot! Onker! These girls were perfectly capable of taking care of themselves. They were soldier women, fighting ladies, Jikai Vuvushis, and now I had them in my juruk—for the guard had taken them in for good.

With the Fifth Phalanx seen safely off to barracks and with the guard trotting at our backs, we set off for the next function of the declining day.

"I could do with a wet, my old dom," said Seg.

"Aye. Even inspecting troops is thirsty work," said Nath.

"The disease is catching," I remarked, and felt no little surprise when they laughed at my comment.

So, laughing, we reined in before a neat little tavern we knew pretty well, The Frog and Jut, and dismounted. Thinking of the juruk jikai—which is one fancy name Kregans have for a guard corps—I was aware that I'd have to make the decision about the kind and number of animals they rode. The guard regiments kept up nikvoves and zorcas. The nikvove, heavy, powerful, is one of the better animals to ride in a thumping, rib-jolting charge, knee to knee. The zorca with his spiral horn is altogether more dainty, short-coupled, exceptionally fast and beautiful. The commanders of ESW and EYJ considered both animals essential. But Vallia was short of riding beasts, juts were difficult to come by in any war, Zair knows, and I had, therefore, to make the decision pretty soon.

The guardsmen dismounted and each jurukker was hell bent on slaking his thirst to the greater glory of Beng Dikkane, the patron saint of all the ale drinkers of Paz.

About to walk up the few steps leading under a brick archway where purple and yellow flowers blossomed exotically under the low rays of the suns, we were halted by the sound of galloping hooves from the street. A rider bolted up to the gate, half fell off and half dismounted, didn't bother with the reins, and came flying across the small courtyard toward us.

As a matter of course half a dozen burly lads of the guard magically appeared before me.

We could all see the man's uniform, a smart affair of crimson and yellow, with tasteful silver lace here and there. We all recognized him as a messenger sent by my chief stylor, Enevon Ob-Eye. In his left fist he clutched a fold of paper. Clearly, therefore, Enevon, who ran the office with meticulous accuracy, had sent me a message. Equally clearly, the lads of the duty squadron were going to keep a very close eye on proceedings.

Well, that is the way of it if an emperor has to have all these fancy bodyguards.

"Let Farren through, Deldar Naghan, if you please."

Although I spoke quite pleasantly, Deldar Naghan, exceedingly large, exceedingly scarlet of face, and exceedingly conscious of his position, bellowed in his exceedingly enormous voice: "Quidang, majister!"

The guards stepped aside and young Farren ti Wovoing walked through. He was still breathless from his gallop through the streets of Vondium to find us.

Now I had in my mind's eye a picture of what had happened. Enevon had probably said: "Take this message to the emperor, young Farren. And—bratch!"

The message was quite possibly of world-shaking importance; far more probably it was just routine. That made no difference. If a message he had to deliver had to go to the emperor, then young Farren, like every other bright spark of the messenger service, would break all the speed records getting it to its destination.

I managed a quirk of the lips which passed for a smile and took the paper.

"Majister—

Nath Naformo, a messenger from Natyzha Famphreon—not the Racters—brings a message he will confide to no one but yourself.

Enevon K.S."*

I crumpled the paper.

"Thank you, young Farren. Do you tell Master Enevon Ob-Eye I will return directly."

With a snapped out acknowledgment, Farren turned himself about and ran off to his zorca. He was a young fellow desperate to make a mark for himself, like so many of them in Vallia, so many . . .

I showed Seg and Nath na Kochwold the paper, and then crumpled it again and stuck it down into a pouch on my belt.

"Say nothing of this, of course."

"All the same," said Seg as we went into the snug of The Frog and Jut, "it rings oddly."

The Racters with their black and white favors had once been the most powerful political party in Vallia. Their insurrection had failed and now what was left of them held the far northwest where they warred against the self-created King of North Vallia northward of them and against Layco Jhansi to the south.

They had previously offered an alliance against Layco Jhansi, as he had offered one against them. I did not think this mysterious messenger was Strom Luthien, who did the dirty work for the Racters in this department.

As we downed the refreshing ale served here by a sweet little Fristle fifi in a yellow apron and her fur brushed to a polish of perfection, Seg went on: "And

---

* K.S. Krell Stylor. Krell is one Kregish word for Chief.

A.B.A.

from old Natyzha Famphreon, herself, personally. Not from the Racter party. I suppose she's still a leading light? Maybe they've thrown her out and she asks your help."

"Would to Opaz someone would slit her throat," was Nath's comment just before he buried his nose into his jug.

"You have to give this Nath Naformo full marks for courage." Seg slugged back a gulp of ale. "Any Racter walking into Vondium is likely to have his throat slit, by the Veiled Froyvil!"

We drank up and then remounted to canter off to the palace where a meal awaited us. Still resplendently dressed, and therefore feeling foolish, I decided to see the messenger from Natyzha Famphreon first. Seg and Nath went with me into Enevon's office where we were shown into a small anteroom. The walls were painted a beige, the ceiling was white, there were two desks and four chairs, and the carpet was quite ordinary, with a flower pattern of intertwined Moonblooms. Nath Naformo rose from a chair as we entered.

"Majister." He started to go into the full incline where he'd scrape his idiot nose on the carpet and stick his rump waggling into the air.

I stopped all that nonsense and said: "Sit down, Koter Naformo, and spit it out."

He looked at me frankly. He was in the Kregan way hard, of a middle-age, I judged, given that Kregans live better than two hundred years, and wore decent Vallian buff. His weapons had been taken from him.

"Majister. I am not a Racter. I am employed merely as an agent, between you and the person who wishes to speak to you."

"More mumbojumbo!" said Seg, blowing out his cheeks.

"Surely you recognize the necessity for a Racter to show circumspection here, kov?"

Seg nodded his handsome head in agreement.

"Well?" I said, and I own my voice made the poor fellow sitting opposite jump. Naformo swallowed down.

"If you will attend the upstairs room at the sign of The Piebald Zorca this evening, the person I represent will await you—alone and unarmed."

Enevon screwed up his one eye at me, and pursed his lips. Despite his seniority, he still managed to get ink on himself. "The Piebald Zorca? H'm, majis, that was well-known as a haunt of the Racters when they held power in Vondium."

"And in a highly unsalubrious part, too," said Nath. As a citizen of Thermin, up in the north midlands, he'd assiduously acquainted himself with Vondium.

This Nath Naformo certainly did have courage.

"Am I to understand you fear to go through fear of treachery—"

"Fear?" yelped out Nath.

"Oh, I'll go," I told Naformo. "And I'll have a couple of squadrons of my lads ready if your principal attempts treachery."

Uncharacteristically it was left to Seg to say what lay in our minds.

"Treachery? That we can deal with. It's this dratted werewolf we've got to look out for."

CHAPTER SIX

NATYZHA FAMPHREON
SENDS A REQUEST

The Piebald Zorca had been rebuilt since the earlier structure had been burned down in the Times of Troubles, but the upstairs room was furnished with a faded glory that reminded one of bygone days. There were even black and white decorations to the cornices. They could, of course, have been merely an artist's fancy . . .

Nath snorted when he saw the decorations, and chucked his wide-brimmed hat down onto the table. Then he sprawled out in a chair and stuck his black boots out.

"Drinks all round, landlord, and sharpish!"

"At once, my lord."

Seg and I stared at the person in the black cloak and wearing a black iron mask who rose at our entrance. He wore no weapons. We were fully armed.

"Would I know you, then, koter?" I made the inquiry in a flat voice.

"You might, majister. When the landlord has served us I will remove the mask."

"Make it so."

The room was illuminated by mineral oil lamps, and their slight tang rankled unpleasantly when compared with the sweet aroma of the samphron oil lamps those with more money could afford. When the landlord, a bulldog-faced Brukaj in an almost clean yellow and green striped apron had retired, we broached the bottles and settled about the table.

With a firm gesture the stranger unhooked the clasps and removed the iron mask.

Well, I knew him. But only slightly.

"Lahal, Strom Volgo."

"Lahal, majister."

He was apim, like me, with stern and austere features, bearing the marks of experience. His nose was full and his lips of the thin variety, yet he was not unhandsome. His eyebrows drew down.

"I serve the kovneva, and hold my lands at her hands. She commands, and I obey."

A strom, which is something like the rank of count here on Earth, may hold estates direct from the emperor or king, and also from a kov, or duke. The dowager kovneva Natyzha Famphreon of Falkerdrin owned vast lands. There were many nobles beholden to her.

"Well, jen," I said, which is the correct way to address a lord in Vallia, "you'd better spit it out."

He was not discomposed. He'd heard of me, right enough, since the days when the Racters believed I was merely a propaganda prince, a puffed-up bladder of nothing.

"I have to inform you that the kovneva believes she will soon die—"

"Ha!" exclaimed Nath. "Then you do bring good news!"

Strom Volgo took no notice outwardly; but I noticed his forehead crinkled just a trifle. This man served old Natyzha, and was well aware of the upheavals that would follow the death of a noble.

"She is aware of the enmity shown you by the Racters. She calls to your remembrance her enclosed garden, and the chavonths that escaped and would have killed her and her friends. She grieved, then, that you and she stood in enmity, one against the other."

I said, "I did what was necessary. But I, also, remind her that her son, Nath Famphreon, stood shoulder to shoulder with me. And he was armed only with a rapier."

That had been a blood-stirring little scene, the escaped chavonths, ferocious hunting cats, leaping out ravenous to kill and eat us. Yes, I'd always felt that Natyzha's son, Nath, was not the ninny everyone thought him. His mother was so powerful, so overriding, so intemperate in her demands, that young Kov Nath vanished in her shadows.

As Strom Volgo went on speaking I realized we were handling high politics, secret understandings, the stuff of which empires are made.

He unhooked the black cloak and tossed it over the back of a chair. He wore Vallian buff, and his long black riding boots were still splashed with mud. He'd come a goodly way southward from Falkerdrin, which lies north of the Black Mountains and north of Vennar, over the River of Rippling Catspaws. My blade comrade Inch was still fighting to regain control of his Black Mountains, and my comrade—never a blade comrade!—Turko was struggling to hold onto his new kovnate of Falinur and to hook left into Vennar whose borders marched westward of him. And, of course, Vennar was the kovnate of Layco Jhansi, the old emperor's chief pallan, traitor, forsworn murderer.

"You still fight Layco Jhansi, then, Strom Volgo."

"Of course, to all outward seeming."

I didn't like the sound of this. Neither did Seg. He sat up.

"Oh?"

Volgo spread his hands. He wore the colored favors and symbol—known as a schturval—of Falkerdrin. Black and gold the colors, a chavonth the symbol. The schturval glittered in the oil lamps' glow.

"I have been commanded by the kovneva to tell you whatever you wish to know, majister. She feels she is near death—"

"And is this sooth? Is Natyzha really dying?"

"Yes."

"From all accounts," put in Nath na Kochwold, "her son Nath Famphreon is no man to be a kov. He'll have his head off before he leaves the graveside."

"Yes," said Strom Volgo.

Seg fidgeted away at what had been said earlier.

"What d'you mean, strom, about to all outward seeming you still fight that bastard Layco Jhansi?"

"I have been commanded to tell the emperor all. The Racters have come to an understanding with Layco Jhansi—"

"The devil they have!"

"Aye. The Racters will turn their main efforts against this maniacal King of North Vallia, and Jhansi will in likewise smash this new Kov Turko of Falinur."

"By the Black Chunkrah!" I flamed out. "This is ill news!"

"And it explains why Turko has been having such a bad time recently." Seg gripped his square brown fist onto the smooth shaft of his bowstave. "I'll have to go up there, my old dom, and—"

"Too right! And I'll be with you, and with reinforcements for Turko. The whole front could collapse and then—by Krun! It doesn't bear thinking of!"

Strom Volgo rubbed salt into our wounds.

"Now that Layco Jhansi has access to the sea through Racter territory he has been hiring many mercenaries."

"That does it," declared Seg. He stood up, big, handsome, his dark hair wild, and prowled about the room like a veritable leem.

"My thanks to you, Strom Volgo, and to Natyzha. She has done us a good service with this intelligence. Although—" and here I confess I stroked my chin—"I am at a loss as to why she should so inform us."

"That is why I am here. When the kovneva dies she is confident that the lords of the Racter lands will descend like warvols upon her kovnate. Her son Nath, whom she loves in her own hard fashion, will be swept aside. He will likely be slain. Certainly, she believes, Kov Nath will never inherit Falkerdrin."

"That seems reasonable," said Nath na Kochwold.

But, having had a glimpse of the purpose and steely determination in Natyzha Famphreon, I thought I could see what she wanted. And I stood aghast. I had to let Volgo spell it out, for it was a request I did not wish to hear.

"The Kovneva Natyzha Famphreon of Falkerdrin begs and demands of you, Dray Prescot, Emperor of Vallia, that you guarantee the legal and actual inheritance of her son, the Kov Nath Famphreon of Falkerdrin."

"Do what?" Seg's voice as he stopped pacing and swung about, head jutting, was a snarl. "Is the woman insane?"

"She has, Kov Seg, taken the measure of the emperor. This request cannot be dealt with by anyone else."

Quite mildly, I said: "If I accede to this astonishing request, and I send—or, rather, ask—Kov Seg Segutorio, to go up to Falkerdrin and sort it all out, then, believe you me, Volgo, Kov Seg will sort it all out—and in a most handsome way, by Vox!"

Volgo blinked his eyes twice, rapidly.

"I'll go like a shot, of course, Dray. But I own I'm a damned sight more worried over Turko."

"So am I. Turko's problems with this Imp of Sicce Jhansi are far more pressing than Natyzha's presentiments of death."

"Your pardon, majister—but the kovneva really is dying. The needlemen and puncture ladies are helpless."

"Well, Volgo, I'll think about it. You have to admire the old biddy, though. She was always the toughest nut of all the Racters. When—"

"Majister!" He interrupted with full knowledge of what often used to happen to folk who interrupted emperors when they were talking. "I crave your pardon. But the kovneva is dying, and she must have your positive answer to comfort her on her death bed. I am sure you can see that—majister."

"I see you are devoted to her, Volgo, and that I admire. Very well. Take back this word. I have a good memory of Kov Nath—no, by Krun!—I have an affection for that young man. I shall do all I can do to see he is not defrauded of his estates, and that he is not slain. But if all this happens when I am not there, or my armies have not broken through, why, then. . . ."

"You will contrive it, majister. That is why my mistress sent this request."

Knowing Seg of old I tried not to catch his eye. Some hope! His gaze appeared to hook and hold me, to hypnotize me. He laughed that Seg Segutorio laugh.

"There, my old dom! I've told you before." He used Kregish words. But what he was saying was: "You're too much the perfect knight for your own good."

I had to react.

"Perfect knight! By Zim-Zair! After all the strokes we've pulled!"

Nath na Kochwold, good comrade though he was, could only look at us two, lost.

Strom Volgo was most punctilious.

"I shall be happy to carry back your word to my mistress. The dowager kovneva has not had a happy life since the Times of Troubles—"

"Well, by Vox!" exploded Nath. "Who has?"

The ugly meanings of the words hung on the air. The curtains to the tall windows had been drawn, and they were, I recall, of a thick weave from the eastern provinces of Vallia, in a pale gray with silver curlicues. As Nath's intemperate and valid words still echoed in the chamber, a shrill and heartbreakingly terrified scream shrieked outside the windows.

Seg and I were shoulder to shoulder at the window. He ripped the drapes aside. We stared out into the moons-drenched night.

The small courtyard lay directly beneath us. Men of the guard were running out, drawing their swords. The wall confining the courtyard from the street hid their view. But we could see—we could see over the wall and into the narrow alleyway where between overhanging balconies and frowning façades, the cobbles glistened in a narrow streak where the moons-light reached down.

"There!" shouted Seg.

Nath stood at our shoulders, peering out. He yelled, angrily, incensed, violently: "The damned ganchark!"

A lean loping form of shaggy gray fur leaped along the street and in the evil thing's mouth the limp form of a girl showed horridly that he had found and killed his prey.

Now the werewolf was carrying his victim off to devour her at his leisure.

CHAPTER SEVEN

OF THE ABSENCE OF BLOOD AND FUR

No other man in two worlds could have done it. Of that I am perfectly sure.

Seg's bow snugged in his hand, where he had been polishing up the shaft as we talked. Now the bow snapped up, the arrow slashed from the quiver, the shaft was nocked, the bow bent, all in so smooth and wondrous a fashion as to amaze any young coy newly recruited into an archer regiment—as to amaze me, by Vox!

Seg loosed.

The werewolf, clearly visible by the fuzzy pink moonlight of The Maiden with the Many Smiles, leaped for the corner. The girl dangling from his jaws flopped about as the ganchark bounded on. The lethal gray form, spikey with menace, angular in motion and yet flowing with evil grace, rounded the corner and vanished.

Seg said: "I don't believe it."

Nath started to say something, stopped, cleared his throat, and then turned back. He went over to the table and poured himself a glass of red wine. His hand did not shake; I had the feeling that had it done so I would not have been surprised.

Seg shook his head.

"I hit him."

He turned to me, and his handsome face was cast in as serious a mold as I'd ever seen it. "Dray—you know I do not boast over shooting, for that is folly. But when I hit, I know I hit. I hit that beast."

"I believe you, Seg. Let us go down and find out."

"The shaft should have taken him just below his forequarters, straight through. It would have pierced his heart."

Nath said: "There is no reliable evidence to prove that gancharks have hearts."

"Then he would have been hit sore. He would not have bounded on so fleetly—"

"Let's go down," I said, again.

The thing was unnerving. Seg knew when he hit. When a mortal being was struck by a clothyard shaft, fletched with the rosy feathers of the Zim-Korf of Valka, tipped by hardened steel, that being was struck through. And if Seg said he'd hit so as to pierce the heart, that mortal being was dead.

Dead.

The other answer to that equation rang evilly in my old vosk-skull of a head.

The jurukkers of the guard knew what they were about and the guardsmen fanned out past the gateway, covering the cross street as well as the one along which we now hurried. The Twins, eternally orbiting each other and throwing down their mingled light, joined the Maiden with the Many Smiles to drown the alleyway in pink radiance.

Two guards sprinted back toward us, and because they were of the Emperor's Sword Watch their equipment did not jingle and jangle. The leader, a kampeon, saw me and yelled.

"Majister! The shaft!"

He reached us, slapped to a halt and held out Seg's arrow. I took it.

"Thank you, Diarmin. There was no blood?"

"Not a drop, as Vikatu is my witness."

I handed the shaft to its owner.

"Well?"

Seg Segutorio is a man of parts. He took the shaft between his powerful fingers, twirled it, checked the flights, and then he lifted the bright steel head to his nose and sniffed.

"Oiled steel," he said. "Nothing else."

The youngster paired off with the old sweat Diarmin and being instructed by him in soldierly virtues, had that clean-cut, pink, shining face that is so heart-breakingly vulnerable beneath the harsh iron brim of the helmet.

Now he swallowed down with a gulp, and said: "I think—majister—I thought—"

Diarmin had served with me for a long time and knew my ways, and what he could get away with. He bellowed: "Spit it out, jurukker! Do not keep the emperor waiting!"

"It was me who found the arrow, majister. When I picked it up I thought—that is—"

"Untangle your tongue, jurukker!" fairly foamed Diarmin, crimson that he was thus being shown up in front of his emperor.

"Yes, Deldar Diarmin—There was a tiny scrap of gray fur on the arrowhead—"

"Fur! Fur! Well, young Nairvon, where is it now?"

"I—I don't know—"

"Dropped it, did you! Lost valuable evidence! That's a charge for you, my lad. You'll jump in the morning when the Hikdar sinks his teeth into you!"

"Yes, Deldar."

"Now just a minute," put in Seg. He waggled his arrow. "You're positive there was a scrap of fur, Nairvon?"

"Yes, Kov Seg—well, almost certain."

Deldar Diarmin opened his mouth and Seg got in first—just—

"But you didn't drop it, did you?"

"No, jen, no. It was evidence."

I said, "Deldar Diarmin, why don't you and the jurukker go back up the alleyway with torches and look?"

"Quidang!" Diarmin's voice boomed and rattled against the gray walls. "Jurukker Nairvon—*bratch*!"

The two guardsmen started off and Seg shouted after them: "Get some more of your comrades on the job."

Nath na Kochwold had remained silent during this interchange. Now he drew a breath.

"I do not like to disbelieve in the word of young Nairvon. If Seg shot a wolf, and there was fur clipped off, then Nairvon dropped the evidence."

Seg said, "But?"

"Ah, yes. If it was a werewolf then you might have clipped a considerable quantity of fur. But it would not be found."

"And no blood."

"Quite."

The incongruousness of this military protocol, the Deldar bellowing, the youngster stammering, the feel of routine and orders and a settled way of life, when viewed against the eerie happenings, the breath of occult horror, struck me shrewdly. I did not think this damned werewolf was going to be dealt with in Standing Orders.

With that old intemperate rasp in my voice, I said,

"Let's get back and finish this business with Strom Volgo."

My comrades agreed, and Nath said quietly: "I don't think they'll find any fur."

"And I hit the beast, of that I am sure."

"So that, Seg, as you hit what you shoot at, and the beast was not slain and did not drop blood . . ." Nath shook his head. "This is going to be a bad business."

"We must find out who that poor girl was." I could still see that pathetic figure with dangling arms and legs, the white dress like a moth's wing, clamped in the jaws of the wolf.

"And," said Seg with a most ugly note in his voice, "what the hell she was doing out alone."

When we returned to the upstairs room of The Piebald Zorca Strom Volgo had donned his black iron mask.

No doubt, I thought and my comrades must also have reasoned, he had decided this was none of his business.

The order of importance, as I saw it, of what lay ahead of us was: Firstly, to reinforce Turko and hold the front, and conjointly with this to ascertain the situation of Inch. Secondly, to deal with this werewolf; and, thirdly, to do what could be done for Natyzha Famphreon and her son Nath.

This I explained to Strom Volgo.

"I must accept the needle in this, majister. For I see your position. I rest content that you have given your word."

Seg pulled his chin at this, but the deed had been done and there was no gainsaying it.

"Strom Volgo," I said, halting him as he took his

leave. "Allow me to send a half-squadron to see you safely out of Vondium."

He hesitated. Then—"As you wish, majister. And my thanks."

A sensible fellow, then . . .

In pursuance of the decision on precedence I had a perfect instrument to carry out the first task with me now in the shape of Nath na Kochwold. We went off back to the palace with the guard trotting along after, and I was half-amused to see they rode with bared weapons. If Seg shot the damn thing and it didn't drop dead, then these fine lads wouldn't do much better . . .

"Nath," I said. "About Turko—"

"Ha! You want me to—"

"I want you to finish off training the Fifth Phalanx." He glowered at me.

"Very well. As you know, there is only one thing I like better than training a phalanx, and that is leading it in battle."

"You're a bloodthirsty villain, all right, Nath."

"Oh, aye, sometimes."

We'd rearranged the distribution of the various Phalanxes—or, rather, they had been rearranged when I'd been away from Vallia. The half-phalanx, or wing, we seldom thought of in those terms, that is, of being a half, rather, we thought of the wing as the Kerchuri, a unit in its own right two of which formed a single Phalanx. The whole phalanx corps was thus organized.

I told Nath na Kochwold what I intended.

"I shall take the Sixth Kerchuri with me up to Turko. Vondium will be safe with the Ninth and Tenth."

The Third Phalanx had a special place in our affections. The Sixth Kerchuri of the Third had been the unit to move into line and plug the gap when the savage clansmen astride their voves had almost broken through at the Battle of Kochwold. From that battle Nath took his name.

"Very well. After all, the Fifth is not really a green outfit. Plenty of the men served in the old Fifth."

"Good."

"And when you call on us I'll bash a little more knowledge into 'em when we march up to join you."

"As to that, Nath, I would hope to clear this problem without calling on you. Drak down in the southwest might call. And up in the northeast past Hawkwa country—"

Seg said gruffly, "We do well up there, Dray."

"Aye," confirmed Nath. "It's mostly light troops to ride to counter raids. There is a case to be made for withdrawal of a Kerchuri."

I said, "Talk it over with Farris."

Truth to tell, it was these confounded girls who worried me. No matter how many times I told myself that I was just being plain stupid, I still felt that uncomfortable itch when I saw a Warrior Maiden in action. They looked splendid striding about in their tall black boots, with their long legs limber and lithe, their faces glowing with health, their eyes bright. That was all the façade, the parade, the fancy uniforms, the trumpets pealing, drums hammering and the flags flying.

The reality of action, of blood and death were far removed from the fairy-tale romance of the Jikai Vuvushis.

The palace was alive with lights when we returned. No one intended to be caught by a werewolf in the uncanny shifting shadows.

Garfon the Staff, our respectable and highly efficient majordomo, told me that Deb-Lu-Quienyin was waiting in the reception room outside my private quarters. Delia was not there, and she had left me a note, and Deb-Lu-Quienyin, answering the urgent request to return to Vondium had had a tiring flight.

We went straight through shouting for wine and throwing off our capes. Deb-Lu smiled when he saw us and ceased from his pacing about the Walfargweave rugs.

"Lahal, Deb-Lu. You've heard all about this werewolf?"

"Lahal, majis—aye. A bad business. But there are ways and means."

"Too right," said Seg, seizing up a glass and looking around for the nearest bottle.

You will notice the way Deb-Lu and we spoke—no tiresome formalities, no swaths of lahals and majisters and polite inquiries after health. None of that at this fraught moment in Vondium's history. Yet Deb-Lu and I had not seen each other for a long time—a damn long time, by Krun!

"Now that is what I expected to hear," I exclaimed, taking the glass from Seg. "Although, San, there is still a chance that this beast is not a werewolf."

Almost every time I see Deb-Lu-Quienyin in my mind's eye and recall him with affection and awe, I seem inclined to say that he looked just the same. Well, of course he did, and yet looked changed at certain times. As a famed and feared Wizard of Loh, addressed as San, he was a member of the small band of brothers and sisters clustered about the emperor and empress. I was about to say a respected and valued member; but all the folk in that fellow and sistership were respected and valued.

No. There is still no doubt in my mind that of all

the sorcerers on Kregen, the Wizards of Loh rank very very high. As you may be aware, I had only slowly been growing aware of their true powers. Looking at Deb-Lu now and feeling that familiar surge of affection for him, I saw he had taken off his enormous turban. His red Lohvian hair looked disheveled. He was your very figure of a powerful mage, and yet there were no runes embroidered upon his robes, no massive array of skulls and feathers and books. The Wizards of Loh were long past the need for material artifacts to assist in casting a spell.

He did have a staff. It stood propped against a chair. Deb-Lu used to say to me that he really had the staff to assist his weary old bones to hobble about—as you will see he liked to put on the pretense of advancing years in a most unKreganlike way. He must have picked up a deal of his complaining routine from old Hunch . . .

And that reminds me that there are a whole lot of folk living and working in Vondium who deserve a mention at this time, and yet whom I must for the moment abandon as the unfolding story of the Werewolf of Vondium takes precedence.

What Deb-Lu said was short, succinct—and pretty damn obvious, by Zair, had we listened and used our heads for something else than hanging pretty-feathered hats on.

"Dudinter," said Deb-Lu-Quienyin. "Dudinter."

CHAPTER EIGHT

THE FOUR SMITHS

Emder, sober-faced, lifted the statue. Emder, sober-minded, meticulous, supremely efficient, is the friend who looks after me when I happen to be in a palace or a civilized place, as Deft-Fingered Minch, my crusty old kampeon comrade, is the friend who looks after me in camp. Now Emder shook his head.

"It is a great pity. The piece has merit."

"Aye," Seg said with some emphasis, and gave Emder no chance of holding onto the statue by tweaking it out of his grasp.

"What the empress will say . . ." started Emder. Then he halted. "No. I am being foolish. The empress would command instantly that her girls remove what is necessary from her own boudoir and anywhere else."

"You are right, Emder," I said, and reached out for a candlestick, one of a pair, and Seg, hurling the statue into the sack, went over and fetched the other candlestick. Both went clink into the sack.

"Although," said Nath na Kochwold, "if you asked the citizens of Vondium to contribute, they would do so willingly and to the best of their ability."

"They've suffered enough, what with all the wars and destruction. If the palace here cannot find enough then I'll loot some other damned place I'm supposed to own."

On this Earth a couple of thousand years or so ago Pliny described electrum as consisting of one part of silver to four of gold. Native gold dug up with something approaching a half admixture of silver, not less than a fifth, was also reasonably common on Kregen; but we did not have time to go prospecting. To find the quantities of electrum we needed we simply grabbed all the statues and pretty little objects fabricated from dudinter and used them.

Garfon the Staff came in, belted his golden-banded balass staff down and said in what was for him a very soft whisper: "The four smiths are here, majister!"

"Right. I'll see 'em now. Get all this stuff down to the forges right away." Briskly, I strode off and as I went I tweaked a neat little dudinter trinket from a side table. This was a miniature of those enormous statues that come from Balintol, of an eight-armed person, a Talu, dancing with fingers outstretched like an abandoned cartwheel.

The attractive pale yellow color of electrum, named for amber in the old Greek, glimmered in my hand as I went off to the reception room. The four smiths stood a trifle uneasily, summoned by the emperor to the palace. I hoped not a one of them was uneasily running through his mind the list of his latest crimes!

Well, the job was simple enough.

"We have to rid ourselves of this ganchark, my friends. And to do that we have to stick him with a weapon forged from dudinter. Arrow piles—and the broad fleshcutters particularly. Swords and spears. You'll have to get an edge the best way you can."

"We will forge an edge, majister," said Naghan the Bellows, the armorer.

Ortyg Ortyghan, the goldsmith, nodded eagerly. Logan Loptyg chipped in to say that he would work night and day. He was the silversmith.

The foxey Khibil face of Param Ortygno expressed confidence, and also caution.

"I am the dudinter smith you have summoned, majister. Maybe the chief place should be given to me, for, after all, we are to work in my specialty and I am a Khibil." At that he brushed up his arrogant whiskers, a true-blue haughty fox-faced Khibil to the life.

I did not laugh.

"I am grateful to you for your willing offer of help, Koter Ortygno. The fate of Vondium is at stake in more ways than perhaps you may imagine. I think it best if you four work in harmony, as a team, like a quadriga. There should be no need for any professional secrets to be revealed. Those parts of the work may be conducted as each one of you sees fit." I fixed them with an eye that has often, most unkindly, been described as a damned baleful Dray Prescot eye. "Am I understood?"

"Understood, majister!" they sang out in a chorus. "*Queyd arn tung!*"*

They each gave a respectful little nod of the head and turned to leave. If sometimes I overreact to all this bowing and scraping and condemn it too harshly, I hope the reason is not some deep psychological flaw in me that demands and rejects an attention I cannot bring into the open lights of day. Those four little nods of the head I reasoned showed proper respect not for me as a man but for my position. It was to the emperor the respect was due, who repre-

*Queyd-arn-tung! No more need be said.—A.B.A.

sented Vallia. These men had been among those clamorous crowds who had called me and elected me emperor to sort out their troubles. If a fellow or a girl cannot feel respect for their own country, then the world may not roll around.

Of course, that brings up the knotty problem of what happens when your country falls below the standards you consider to be proper and decent in the world . . .

I became aware of the little dudinter statue in my hand. I called after the four smiths.

"Wait, my friends."

They turned at once and I threw the Talu toward them. Interestingly enough, it was not the haughty Khibil, Param Ortygno, who caught the thing. He might be the dudinter smith; but it was Naghan the Bellows who took the eight-armed idol out of the air and without a scratch.

"Remberee," I said.

"Remberee, majister."

Delia's note merely said she'd been called away to the bedside of a dying friend. She did not name the friend.

I thought I knew.

The sorority to which Delia belonged, the Sisters of the Rose, was in any terms a powerful Order. Much of their work was carried on in the open; a very great deal remained secret. Through the surprising favor of the Star Lords, I had been afforded the privilege of vicariously sharing in some of Delia's adventures, discovering thereby many secrets Delia would never reveal to a man, and, also thereby, feeling honor-bound to keep them totally concealed. In fact, I never thought about them if I could manage that trick.

One fact, however, I did know. The mistress of the Order, who had once been known as Elomi the Shining, from Valka, was dying. Delia had been chosen to be the next mistress, and had refused. The Sisters of the Rose were in every sense important; for Delia being Empress of Vallia was also important in an entirely different fashion, a fashion in which the idea of obligation and service figured in just as dramatic a way as it did in the Sisters of the Rose.

So, I knew Delia had gone to Lancival. The location of this place, so secret and unknown, remained a secret as far as I was concerned, even although I could laugh with glee along with the SOR at the impudence of the place's disguise in Vallia. There Delia would confer with her peers, politic with some, cajole others, argue, plead, seldom order—although that she could do supremely well, by Vox!—and eventually they would elect the new mistress.

If by some mischance some feminine chicanery landed Delia with the job, I fancied she'd make a different kind of mistress of the SOR from any hitherto in the Order's long history.

All our daughters had been educated and trained by the SOR, as our sons by the Krozairs of Zy. I devoutly believe there is no better education or training anywhere in two worlds.

Because something of that kind had been flowing through my mind when the outlying islands of Vallia had been attacked by the reiving fish-headed Shanks from over the curve of the world, we'd formed an Order, originally in Vallia, based on the Krozairs of Zy. The mystical and superhuman woman we knew as Zena Iztar had been instrumental in aiding us to get the new Order, the Kroveres of Iztar, formed and aware of the fact that it was in the process of creating a tradition for the future.

Seg Segutorio was the Grand Master of the KRVI.

Where there was injustice, where tyranny, where we were attacked by the Shanks, there—in theory— the brothers of the KRVI would be found assisting the oppressed and resisting the Shanks.

A new and what was, I suppose, a daring idea had recently been giving me some interesting prospects for future action.

Why not, I'd said to myself, why shouldn't both men and women join the same order and fight injustice, succor the weak and helpless, fight the damned fish-headed Shanks?

Well, it was a thought . . .

At this point it is proper for me to mention that I knew very little of the other female Orders of Paz. The Sisters of the Sword, the Sisters of Samphron, the Grand Ladies, the Little Sisters of Opaz, and many others were secret still.

I did know that a new Order, the Sisters of the Whip, had collapsed.

So when Seg joined me the first thing I said was: "It seems to me that this damned werewolf is a suitable job for the kroveres."

"By the Veiled Froyvil, my old dom! You are right!"

"We have lost touch a little lately, of course."

"Well, we've been off in Pandahem. But—let me see—" and although Seg's fey blue eyes did not actually cross in thought, his face took on a most menacing expression as he mentally began sorting out the brothers available to undertake this mission.

In this my narrative of my life on Kregen there are many people who appear illuminated, as it were, in the forefront of the action, only to subside into the background as fresh events overtake us. But these folk were not forgotten. They formed the living breathing fabric of life and friendship. Many of them met and talked with me almost every day. Others I saw at banquets, dinners, rowdy parties or within the harsher environs of business, the church, the law and the army.

Unmok the Nets, for instance was—still—undecided what business to undertake next. The Pachak twins still cared for Deb-Lu-Quienyin. Our Khibil wrestlers had found ready employment, going eventually with Turko. Tilly and Oby were a permanent part of life. And—Naghan the Gnat. As I said to Seg: "We didn't hoick our friends out of the Arena in Huringa for nothing. Naghan can start fashioning dudinter weapons right away."

Seg said: "Do wha—? Oh, yes, surely. I can put my finger on a score of brothers within a day. And, as for Naghan the Gnat, I am more than happy to wield any weapon made by him."

"Good."

"Although it is a pity Vomanus is still poorly."

"He is taking more time to recover than I like. But he will. He has, like us, bathed in the Sacred Pool of Aphrasöe."

"Don't remind me. I am still totally confused by all the implications—"

"You are not alone!"

"That's as may be. His daughter, Valona, turned up pretty sharpish, so I heard, after Delia sorted out the trouble up in Vindelka."

"Sister of the Rose, business conducted by these formidable women to our confusion. There was a time when I sincerely believed that Valona was my daughter Lela—"

"If I made some humorous remark about that's what you get for chasing off to the ends of Kregen, then I'd be a dolt. Now I know about your comical little Earth with only a yellow sun and only one moon and no diffs, I can understand a lot more that you've never spoken of."

"You can? Maybe, Seg my Bowman comrade, it is time for us to try a few falls on the mat."

"You can take on Korero the Shield. I'm off to find Balass the Hawk and start this werewolf thing moving."

"Korero?"

"Drak has sent the First Regiment of the Emperor's Sword Watch back to Vondium. Well—" and here Seg laughed in his rip-roaring raffish way"—he couldn't hold on to them for a single heartbeat when they learned you were back in Vondium!"

"No," I said. "No, that rascally bunch will insist on putting their bodies between me and danger."

Although I spoke flippantly, I felt the leap of spirits at this news. 1ESW might be a rascally bunch, the regiment was also a smashingly powerful fighting instrument, devoted, very much a law unto itself in matters of regimental honor and pride, and still a unit of the army, standing shoulder to shoulder with their comrades in the defense of Vallia.

Seg moved off and called back: "They'll want to go with us up to Turko, Dray."

"Yes. I shudder to think what 2ESW will say . . ."

CHAPTER NINE

WEREWOLF
AT THE PARTY

I draw a merciful veil over the uproarious happenings when my lads of 1ESW flew into Vondium.

By Vox! Carouse! They did not quite tear the place to bits, but they beat up the city sorely.

They were all there, thanks to the mercy of Opaz, and while some had taken wounds, all were recovered. There were new members of the regiment, of course, and it was my task to get to know them all as quickly as possible. No one entered the ranks of the premier guard regiment unless he was a proven kampeon, a swod of merit, a superb fighting man.

They decided they'd better have some kind of formal parade, and march through the streets to the Temple of Opaz Militant, and there render up thanks. The bands played, the flags fluttered, the suns glinted off massed ranks of armor and weapons. The spectacle delighted the crowds who turned out in their thousands to cheer. The rogues had even organized a bevy of pretty young girls, half-naked sprites in silken draperies all a-swirling, to dance ahead and scatter flower petals. That made me give a grotesque tweak of the lips which my friends recognized as a smile.

Not one of them, nobody, not a single swod, got drunk. I have explained how that kind of idiotic anti-social behavior was not tolerated in the guard corps.

Targon the Tapster, Cleitar the Smith who was now Cleitar the Standard, Ortyg the Tresh, Volodu the Lungs, all of them were there. Korero the Shield, a magnificent sight as always, a golden Kildoi with four arms and a tail hand, uplifting his shields in protection, Dorgo the Clis, saturnine and with his facial scar a livid blaze, and Naghan ti Lodkwara together with all our other comrades from the original Choice Band joined by our new fellows marched in the streaming mingled lights of the Suns of Scorpio.

Vondium, the proud city, as the capital of Vallia is a civilized metropolis of a civilized country. Yet, as I watched the parade and marveled afresh at the panache and bearing, the spirit and devilment of the jurukkers of 1ESW, I could not fail to be aware of the barbaric appearances everywhere, the feeling of passions bursting through regimentation, the savage warrior spirits chafing at and yet understandingly accepting discipline. Mazingle, the swods call that on occasions, and sometimes they call unfair and too harsh a discipline mazingle, with darker and far more ugly meanings.

For a brief moment a vision of the zazzers of the Eye of the World, the inner sea of the continent of Turismond, took my inner attention. Drunkenness was more common among both Grodims and Zairians there, although still generally regarded as the pastime of the feeble-minded. The zazzers were those folk—both men and women, apim and diff alike—who quaffed until they reached a fighting frenzy before battle. Unlike the old Norse berserkers, who either wore bear skins or stripped naked, according to your sources, they smashed into action fully

accoutred and armed, ragingly high seas over, roaringly
sloshed, and fought until they won or were cut down.
The zazzers' philosophy may appeal to many; as a
shortcut to personal extinction it repelled more.

A tremendous shindig was held that night, the
torches flared their orange and golden hair, the sweet
scents of moonblooms mingled with that of exotic
foods and enormous quantities of wines. While we
might not have shaken the stars, we surely shook all
Vondium.

As I say, I draw a decent and merciful veil over
the proceedings.

After the orchestra in their platform-shell at one
side of the flower garden had played the Imperial
Waltz of Vallia, which as you know was the best
rendering I could contrive of the Blue Danube, and
the folk had danced the whole sequence three times
over, I spotted young Oby.

Well, I should not refer to him as young Oby, of
course, for he was a grown and limber man. Two
girls clung to his arms, another rode his shoulders
and waved a bottle aloft, and a fourth in some mysterious way held on with her naked legs wrapped around
his waist from the front, and was busily kissing him
in between laughing and drinking. He saw me and,
disengaging his mouth from its amorous combat, grimaced and called across.

"I cannot help it!"

Oby ran the Aerial Squadron attached to the palace,
and always seemed to be in peril of sudden and
immediate marriage, which with a sleight of hand
much admired among the raffish bloods and despaired
of by the maidens, never was—in his words—trapped.

"I would feel envy, Oby, but for good reasons!"

"Aye, Dray, aye! Would that I could find—" and then he was devoured again.

I yelled: "Where's Naghan?"

Oby twisted his head and the girl's lips sizzled down his cheek. She started to bite his ear—of course.

"In the armory—he's finishing up the first of the arrowheads."

"Then," declared Seg briskly, "that's where I'm off."

"I'll join you."

The palace jumped. Lights festooned the alleyways between hedgerows of sweet-smelling shrubs, lamps twinkled in the trees as a tiny zephyr trembled the branches. It was a glorious night, with She of the Veils flooding down her roseately golden radiance.

"I could wish Milsi was here," said Seg. "But she has gone off with Delia."

"Ah! That means, I would guess, your Milsi is about to be inducted into the Sisters of the Rose." I shot my comrade a hard glance. "I don't know if you should be congratulated or consoled, by Krun!"

"Young Silda never had any doubts."

"Your daughter, and my son ought really to sort things out—Silda is down in the southwest, I suppose?"

"Aye."

We strode through the various gardens and arbors until we'd skirted this side of the palace and so crossing a graveled drive walked up to Naghan's armory.

Naghan the Gnat had once been all gristle and bone; now he had filled out a trifle and his thin and wiry form filled his tunic to greater effect. Amazingly cheerful, quick and lively, he could bash his hammer on his anvil with consummate skill. He is among the finest of the armorers I have known on Kregen. Now he turned as we entered, feeling the heat from the furnace, and he held up between iron tongs a palely yellow arrowhead.

"The edge is the art of it," he said. "Seg—there are a full score over there for you."

"Well done, Naghan," I said. "And a sword?"

Naghan had worked damned hard, that was clear. He had taken the pattern of sword called a drexer which we had developed in Valka and knocked out three of them. His assistants were hard at it, bellows pumping, heat pulsing, hammers ringing, and the hissing turbulence and aromas of quenching going on neatly within the armory. Picking up a dudinter drexer I swung it about experimentally.

"Nolro!" yelped Naghan. "Fetch the quiver."

A young lad, streaming sweat to the waist, jumped to a peg and fetched down the quiver. This was a simple, plain quiver as issued to the archers of the army. Nolro handed it to Seg. It contained a score of arrows, fletched with the rose-red feathers of the zim korf of Valka.

"I had Lykon the Fletcher do these up for you, Seg," explained Naghan. "Speed is the watchword now."

Seg drew out an arrow. It lacked a point. "Thank you, Oh Gnat. I trust Lykon's handiwork. But—"

We all knew Seg liked to build his arrows himself. He now meant that he'd accept another's work in fletching the shafts, but was pleased to bind on the heads himself. This he at once started to do, there and then, at a side bench where the necessary equipment had been prepared.

The party still racketed away among the gardens of the palace. There were Jikai Vuvushis there, out of uniform, dressed exquisitely, laughing, dancing. I own I felt an ache that Delia was not here.

Still, she was removed from the lurking menace of the werewolf. That thought made me speak out, and somewhat bombastically, I confess, saying, "Now let the damned werewolf show his ugly snout." I shook the dudinter drexer. "We'll have his tripes!"

"Aye," confirmed Seg, looking up, holding the first completed arrow. "Aye, my old dom, we'll puncture him like a pincushion."

A shape skulking past the doorway by a clump of pale blue flowers in the torchlights caught the corner of my eye. I swung about. Seg was hard at it pointing up his shafts, but Naghan caught my movement and squinted out into the torchlights across the yard. He wheezed his infectious laugh and swung back to his work, saying; "Well, Dray, you must expect all that, being an emperor and no longer a kaidur!"

"Aye, Naghan, by the Glass Eye and Brass Sword of Beng Thrax himself! But it irks at times . . ."

The skulking shape flicked a red cape back and, seeing he was discovered, walked forward sturdily. Oh, yes, the lads of ESW and EYJ were on duty when the emperor wandered abroad.

"Hai, Erclan!" I called, and I own my voice sounded mocking even in my own ears. "You'd have been shafted for a certainty then, my lad, and well you know it!"

He looked downcast, a young, strong, eager jurukker from 2ESW, knowing he shouldn't have been spotted as he stood watch. I felt for him, for—and if this be boasting then take it as it is meant—there are very few folk, of Kregen or Earth, who can keep an unobserved watch when I do not desire that condition. I did not take pity on him; but I thought to make a small gesture to cheer him up and brace him for the next turn of this kind of duty.

"Look at this, Jurukker Erclan—a fine new blade fashioned from dudinter with which to spill the tripes of the werewolf. Here, try it."

He took the drexer and swung it about. He was from Valka and he addressed me as majister, because he was a youngster and had grown up with that form of address naturally; his father, Emin ti Vinfafn, called me strom—and no messing.

Now Fate plays us all scurvy tricks from time to time and on this occasion I thought I was particularly hard done by—wrongly, as you will hear.

When Naghan first set up his armory for the palace, he, Tilly and Delia felt it would be nice to have shrubs and flower beds not too far away, and to lessen the effect of raw power at work. So the shrubs by which Erclan had lurked and the graveled walks and the flower beds led naturally to other areas of the gardens. A young couple, hands and arms about waists, walked dreamily along, lost to the world in each other. Erclan, swinging the blade, looked across.

"Fodor," he exclaimed in great disgust. "Some people get all the luck and can split the wand, and others have to stand guard duty."

Because of his words I reasoned that the young lady was a bone of contention between the two guardsmen.

About to say something which no doubt would have been highly foolish, I checked. The lethal gray form that flashed into view by the path was no figment of a dream. The foam upon its jaws gleamed in the torchlight. Its eyes reflected the torchlights and speared like two scarlet bolts. Its fur bristled. Undulating with muscle, lethal with fang and claw, the werewolf pounced upon its prey.

"*Fodor!*" screamed Erclan. He flung himself forward.

A single mighty blow from a paw sent Fodor reeling into the bushes. The werewolf hunched above the shrinking form of the girl. Her shriek was lost in the horrid guttural snarls. Erclan, blade high, raced in.

Everything began, happened, and was over.

In a flurry of cape and cords and skidding boots Erclan flung himself bodily at the werewolf. The dudinter blade slashed down.

His body and the flare of the cape obscured the result of his blow. The werewolf shrieked in a hideous screaming whine. It made no further attempt to attack the girl. Erclan lifted the blade again.

The thought scorched into my brain.

"*Now we shall see!*"

The blade flashed, the werewolf snarled and bounded off, Erclan missed and swirled forward. In a few gigantic bounds the werewolf vanished beyond the shrubbery.

Seg stood at my side. He breathed hard.

"What the hell! Erclan hit the beast, I am sure of it—why—?"

I was short, abrupt, hatingly furious.

"The dudinter failed."

CHAPTER TEN

KYR EMDER COOKS DEB-LU-QUIENYIN'S RECIPE

"The electrum blade failed!"

People were running in now and torches illuminated the scene. Erclan bent to the girl, whose long white dress tangled around her legs. We were running across, shouting. The fury that gripped me I know possessed Seg also. We had put store by dudinter to combat this menace, we had believed it would enable us to fight back at the ganchark. And now—this failure, this disaster . . .

Naghan the Gnat came running out clutching his three other dudinter blades. Seg snatched one, I another, and we ran along the path following the trail of the werewolf. We could see blood spots upon the gravel, black coins in the light of the moons.

Guardsmen with torches ran with us. In a mob we raced on.

From up ahead the sound of snarling, whining violence blasted the night air. The horrid sounds ceased, to be followed by a single scream, abruptly choked off. Everyone knew the werewolf had found another victim.

Full of apprehension at what we would find we roared along the path and headed past a graceful circle of lissom trees, past a dell, to burst through bushes onto the path beyond.

A guardsman lay on the path, disheveled, sprawled out, his sword uselessly by his side. Blood streamed from his shoulder, glinting black and red as the torches flared high. He tried to lift his other arm, pointing.

"That way—horrible—horrible—"

"Rest easy," I said, finding the words full of ugly uselessness.

"Fetch a needleman," someone shouted.

Some of the guards started to run on to follow the path; the bloodspots had vanished, disappearing in that magical fashion that had evanished the scrap of fur.

"Hold!" I bellowed. "It is no use chasing farther. The beast is gone. See to Wenerl the Lightfoot here. And all of you, stick close."

"Aye," they said, and looked about uneasily.

The doctors could patch up Wenerl the Lightfoot's body; I wondered what this horrendous experience had done to his mind, his courage, his resolution.

"The girl is safe, majister," said Erclan, panting up. "And Fodor has a cracked rib or two. But—" He saw Wenerl the Lightfoot. "By Vox! The beast struck again!"

I felt it incumbent upon me to attempt to take charge of fears that might slide us all into even greater disaster. What to say? Dudinter had proved false—what else was there we could oppose to this evil that stalked among us, unseen until the moment of death?

"Listen, comrades," I said in a voice only slightly raised. As usual that voice issued forth like an old rusty bucket filled with gravel being dragged up a rocky slope. They all fell silent on the instant. "This evil annoying us in Vondium is merely an evil thing. There will be ways found to destroy it. The wise men, the wizards, they will know. The priests will give us strength. I do not call upon you to have courage; for this you already have, as I well know, for have we not stood shoulder to shoulder on many a battlefield? Keep together, and do not wander off alone. I tell you this, there are no greater sorcerers than the Wizards of Loh, and we have their utmost assistance and advice. Death to the ganchark!"

"Aye," they roared. "Death to the ganchark!"

With that, and feeling mighty small, I can tell you, I went off to have a few words with Deb-Lu-Quienyin. Wenerl the Lightfoot cried out as we vent off: "Hai, majister! Hai, jikai, Dray Prescot!"

As I say, I felt pretty small.

Wenerl was a kampeon, an old hand from 1ESW. On his chest he wore three bobs, and each one of these three medals represented an act of valor. He was a shiv-Deldar and knew his business. His celebrations this night had been unpleasantly interrupted, and I wondered again if the werewolf attack would shake him. I devoutly hoped not. But facing the thundering onslaught of the enemy when they are flesh and blood like you is one thing; facing the ghastly evil of the werewolf was quite another.

Speculation and gossip must now be raging throughout the folk congregated here to have a good time. Rumor would wear a hundred different guises. Hard news would have to be spread, and quickly.

Until I'd learned the meaning of what had transpired from Deb-Lu, the news would remain not hard but soft—damned soft, by Krun.

Walking rapidly at my side along the alleyways between shrubs with torchlights flaring from the trees and the hubbub of the party all about, Seg twisted the shaft between his fingers. His powerful, handsome face looked troubled.

"If the dudinter is of no use, my old dom—then what?"

"Deb-Lu will know. He would not have told us that dudinter was the answer if it was not."

"I agree. Then there is more."

"Evidently."

The Wizard of Loh was not to be found in his own quarters in his own Wizard's Tower. He'd recently accepted the services of two apprentices. These were never going to become Wizards of Loh, of course; but with the level of training afforded by Deb-Lu they could if they studied diligently turn into remarkably qualified and powerful sorcerers. For the moment they fetched and carried, prepared mixtures, hewed wood and drew water, in the old way go-phering for Deb-Lu. One of them, a thin-faced lad with a wart by his nose, which was of the runny kind, looked up as we entered.

"Majister—"

"Where is your master, Phindan?"

"He took Harveng with him, instead of me, and I am to—"

"Where, Phindan, is your master? I have asked you twice."

"Yes, majister, yes. He is with Kyr Emder—"

"The devil he is!"

Seg started off at once, without bothering to lollygag about making footling remarks. I followed. Now what would a puissant Wizard of Loh want with good old Emder?

We found them both in the small kitchen to the side of Emder's quarters where he could supervise personally the preparations of the meals of which he was an expert culinary artist. Everything was spotless. The copper pans glittered in the lamplights. The scrubbed surfaces of the tables gleamed like finest linen. The fires banked to just the right temperature flickered an occasional beam from the grates. The smells were just simply delicious.

Deb-Lu's lopsided turban stood in grand isolation upon a table. He had removed his outer robe and it hung upon a hook behind the door. He and Emder were staring into a copper pot upon the stove, and they were stirring the pot's contents with a long wooden spoon. I sniffed.

"That does not smell like anything I recognize."

Both men turned sharply.

Emder smiled. Deb-Lu, busy, called out: "Jak! Excellent. You have brought the first weapons. You are just in time. Kyr Emder is invaluable in matters of this nature."

I breathed in and breathed out. I thought I understood.

Seg laughed. "So that's the way of it! I am mightily relieved, I can tell you!"

No one else was in the kitchen. I said, "You did not think to put a guard on the door?"

Carefully, Emder said: "We felt that would arouse interest and cause speculation we can do without."

"Yes, you are right."

"Is it ready, San?" Seg walked across and looked into the pot.

"The potion has but now reached the Required Proportions of Evaporation." When Deb-Lu spoke in these clearly heard Capital Letters, matters of import were in the wind.

Seg looked up.

"Potion?"

Deb-Lu sniffed. "Well, yes, Seg, you are quite right. I do not think we will convince the ganchark to open his jaws so that we may pour the liquid down. It will be more in the nature of an injection, by the Seven Arcades, yes!"

He looked around the kitchen, and, quite automatically, put up a hand to push his turban straight, only to discover the absence of that article of headgear.

"I but wait for the return of Harveng. I fear he is almost as idle as his comrade, Phindan; but they must learn hardly if they are to amount to anything in the occult world of thaumaturgy."

Deb-Lu nodded toward a ragged clump of twigs and leaves lying on the floor, striking an incongruous note of untidiness in Emder's immaculate kitchen.

"The lad sorely mistook these plants, when I gave him explicit instructions. Well, well, we were all young once."

Emder gave the mixture a prodding kind of stir.

"If Harveng doesn't return soon, San, I feel— speaking not as a wizard but as a cook—the broth will spoil."

What dire fate would have befallen Harveng we were not to discover, for he pushed the door open and trotted in. He was plump, scarlet-faced, pop of eye and prominent of ear; but he carried a branch ripped from a shrub that made Deb-Lu nod in satisfaction.

"I see I do not have to lose all faith in you, young Harveng. Right, strip the leaves off, and work fast."

This Harveng proceeded to do. With his miraculous aptitude with sharp knife and chopping board, Emder reduced the rolled leaves. His fingertips were tucked in, his knuckles out, and the knife went chop-

chop-chop in a radius, first one way then at ninety degrees. Green juice oozed.

Deb-Lu used an ivory spatula to lift the chopped leaves. He weighed them on his own balance, a spindly construction of balass and ivory, silken-suspended, exact. The required amount went into the pot, and Emder took the wooden spoon and stirred with a nonchalant expert cook's twirl.

Deb-Lu heaved up a sigh.

"This must be kept close, Jak. You know the story of the Ganchark of Therminsax . . ."

"Everyone has heard that dudinter will deal with the werewolf, Deb-Lu. Even the werewolf must have heard—and the vile beast must have laughed, before he struck."

"Oh?"

These two had not heard the uproar, involved as they'd been with the preparation of this potion. We told them what had happened.

"And the girl is safe? And the two lads? By Hlo-Hli—what a moil! I would feel personal guilt had they been killed, for they would have died believing I had betrayed them—"

"Never, Deb-Lu, never. And Wenerl the Lightfoot is no young lad, no green coy, but a kampeon. When he grips a dudinter sword anointed with your potion he will feel very differently, believe me."

"Aye," said Seg. "And that brings up the problem, of course. It's a knotty one."

"How much of this potion is necessary?" I sniffed at the pot. The smell was not unpleasant, with an under flavor of vegetable oil and a tang of bittersweet herbs.

"A single drop is sufficient, given time. But for a more rapid success the more the better up to a

reasonable limit—say a six-inch coating upon a sword—
before any extra becomes unnecessary."

"Then a shaft can do it?"

"Of course, Seg, of course." —

Seg lifted his arrow, looked at the Wizard of Loh,
received a confirmatory nod, and so dipped the arrowhead into the pot. He stirred it about, then withdrew,
flicking off a few drops. The head looked no different
from before.

"That's all very well. But—how do we do it?"

I said, "I had thought, with Deb-Lu's permission,
to involve the various temples in this."

"Ha!" exclaimed Deb-Lu.

"I see that." Seg laid his arrow down and drew the
dudinter sword. "We must keep this secret so that
the werewolf cannot learn it. If the churches bless
the weapons, and anoint them, and folk know they
must have an anointed weapon—yes. It would work!"

"It will work." Deb-Lu turned and glared balefully
upon plump young Harveng. "This is a high secret,
of thaumaturgy and of empire. You will not breathe a
word of what has passed here. If you do I shall know.
Then, I think, you may become—what? A little green
toad? A small brown frog? A slinky shiny slimy worm?"

"No, master, no!" Harveng, plump, scarlet, near-
bursting, sweating, mightily discomposed, stammered
out his protestations. "Never, San, never!"

"So be it!"

Seg, Emder and I remained discreetly silent during this exercise of arcane power.

Then Seg coughed and said: "One thing, San. Steel
did not harm the werewolf, for my shaft just clipped
a little fur, which vanished away. And now we have
this potion to turn dudinter into a proper weapon.

But—what of the dudinter sword with which Erclan struck the werewolf?"

"You are right. Dudinter has power, of itself, to wound a ganchark. It will not really kill the thing, as you say you saw. It will make the beast aware that it can be hurt, drive it off."

Again Deb-Lu put up a hand to push the absent turban straight. He glanced across at me, and then away, and heaved up a sigh, and said: "Mind you, Jak. All this is In Theory Only."

"Oh?"

"Aye, aye. Dudinter—well, that is easy enough. And the potion, too, that is from my childhood. But in fact, in action. No, no, Jak. One Must Wait on Events."

"I see. You've never actually dealt with a werewolf before?"

"Precisely."

"If that blade of Erclan's made the thing run off," I said, "then a wound may be inflicted. A shrewd blow across the neck, say, might lop the beasts head, and—"

"Not quite, Jak. The werewolf by the very nature of the change must involve thaumaturgy of some kind, magic on some level. Steel bounces, as we have seen. Dudinter wounds; but it is generally held that the steel does not bounce, it—"

"How can that be?" said Emder.

"The werewolf possesses regenerative capacity of a very high order. The steel passes through fur, skin, flesh and blood, and instantly the wound heals itself. The moment the steel has passed and the cleavage made, the flesh knits together, the blood circulates."

"Would a severed neck and a lopped head have time to regenerate?"

"Indubitably."

"If the theory is correct . . ." put in Seg. He spoke quietly. I guessed he was wondering what effect an arrow would have, and hating to have to ask.

"Correct or not, we must act on the assumption that San Quienyin's potion will work. There is a lot told in legend and story; we must hold this close."

Deb-Lu got out quite quickly: "Oh, no, Jak. The potion is not mine. I will not tell you its history; but it is named ganjid."

Drawing the dudinter sword I said to Emder: "Have you a pastry brush? You'll get to work to produce more of this ganjid?"

"All day and night, if necessary." He brought across a pastry brush.

"And a vial, a well-stoppered one. A spice phial would do."

Seg and I took turns to paste the ganjid potion onto our sword blades. We laid it on liberally, never mind the six inches that might—or might not—be enough. The liquid sparkled for a moment on the metal and vanished. It did not seem to dry up. It was as though the potion seeped into the metal and was absorbed.

Emder brought a small bottle and this was filled and I popped it into one of my belt pouches. Seg did the same.

"You'll have to contact the four smiths, and Naghan. All the new dudinter weapons will have to be consecrated. I'll get Farris to talk to the chief priests."

"The potion will be ready," promised Deb-Lu.

We four, with Harveng, pop-eyed, looking on, must have presented an odd spectacle. A frighteningly powerful sorcerer, a valet-helpmeet, a formidable Bowman of Loh, and an emperor, standing in a kitchen clustered about a pot on the stove. And I did not forget that that famous Bowman of Loh was a king. We were like a caucus, a cabal, plotting secret doings in dead of night. If anyone had looked in, we'd have appeared downright furtive. We combatted a dark and secret evil, and we were employing dark and secret remedies.

"I'll tell Targon the Tapster and Naghan ti Lodkwara to set an inconspicuous watch. We do not want anyone spying in here." I stretched, scabbarded the sword, took a hitch to my belt. "Now there's an Opaz-forsaken werewolf skulking about out there. I think I'll take a little stroll and see what dudinter and ganjid will do."

As I spoke I felt—and I admit this with no shame, no sense of falling-away—a twinge of doubt.

Would electrum coated with werebane work? Would anything work against the foul pestilence that had fallen on us in Vondium?

I saw Seg looking at me, his head a little on one side. Well, he could guess what I was thinking. Good old Seg! I roused myself.

"I want to have a go at the dratted beast myself first. I believe in your theories, your work, what you have accomplished, Deb-Lu. But—just in case—I don't want some young guardsman, some lad, having his head bitten off and me nowhere around."

Seg let rip a guffaw.

"What! Things happening and Dray Prescot not around! Never . . ."

The others found smiles at this, and I grumped. What I didn't know then was the truth—the awful, horrible truth—behind Seg's chaffing words.

CHAPTER ELEVEN

HOW TWO JURUKKERS STOOD GUARD

Nothing more was seen or heard of the werewolf that eventful night and for the next few days I and my comrades were plunged into hectic activity. There was so much to do. The forces to be taken up to reinforce Turko had to be selected and organized. There were innumerable delegations from all over our part of Vallia to be received and treated honorably, their grievances dealt with as best as possible. Justice had to be delivered. The budget was a constant thorn. Taxes—well, I spare you that blasphemy, for, although as an emperor I needed taxes from the people to pay for everything necessary to run an empire—rickety though that was—I can wince as well as the next fellow when it comes to paying out taxes. Mind you, by Zair, there are taxes and taxes. A just tax to run your country in a proper and decent way—fine. An unjust tax to fatten up the lords—oh, no . . .

Still, I was the emperor and no longer a kind of Robin Hood figure. I used the taxes as wisely as I could, with the Presidio, agonizing over allocations. I refused to have any new building undertaken in the imperial palace and merely maintained what of the fabric was useful. A great deal of the old magnificence was falling into ruin.

We had to put a new wooden roof on one of the outer halls and apartments to house the Jikai Vuvushis Marion was so busily organizing for me.

I know Delia had spoken a soft word, for she did not restrict the recruitment of the new regiment to Sisters of the Sword. For this I was grateful.

"I am mightily intolerant in my choice of girls," Marion told me one fine blustery morning as we set out to check the first consignments of electrum weaponry forged by the four smiths in the city.

Among the glittering throng of riders with us, her affianced man, Strom Nango ham Hofnar, stood out splendidly.

"I am glad to hear it, Marion. Although from what little I know of these ladies, every single one is worth a regiment of mere men."

Her chin went up at this. Well, by Zair! I might not have trembled inwardly for the temerity of my remark, jocular though it was intended to be. I spoke a semi-truth, at the very least. Marion chose to change the subject and comment acidly upon the wind and the raindrops which every now and again spattered upon us.

The four smiths had worked hard and diligently. Guards stood about the stacked weapons. As is the way of these occasions, a crowd gathered to gawp.

"Well done, Smiths all," I said. I shook a thraxter high, trying to get the glimmer of Zim and Genodras to flash along the blade, and finding the dappled clouds too clustered, the rain beginning to spitter down in earnest. "See the weapons are all carefully taken to the temple. Orders will be received from the Lord Farris."

"Yes, majister."

The little scene, damp and cloudy, did nothing to

cheer me up. By the disgusting diseased intestines and foul stinking armpit of Makki Grodno! Oh, I was in a right state, fretting over the safety of Vallia, itching to get off to Turko and having a bash at Layco Jhansi, cogitating how poor old Natyzha Famphreon's problems could be turned to the advantage of Vallia, feeling the pressure of many another thorny problem I have not mentioned to you. And Delia was away somewhere. Yes, as they say on Kregen, I had to accept the needle in all this.

One thing intriguing me I wished to ask Delia.

"Why," I would say after sufficient time had passed for the very necessary greetings to be suitably dealt with, "why is the new imperial guard regiment being formed from a cadre of Sisters of the Sword? Why did you not specify Sisters of the Rose? It is a mystery to me."

Well, the sooner I got the answer the better. Not, as you will readily perceive, because I'd get the answer sooner—oh no!—but because it would mean I'd be with Delia.

The day chosen for the consecration of the weapons was The Day of Opaz Sublime in Glory. Every single day, of course, has its own name. When different religions are involved then a single day may sag heavily under a burden of names.

Other religions were involved, and anxious to give their benedictions. I will spare you the listings of their names and the names of their days.

Suffice it to say, the populace crowded around to see the new dudinter weapons blessed. The priests performed their parts well. Trumpets pealed. Flags fluttered and cracked, for the day continued the blustery weather. Clouds massed and blotted out the light of the suns. Rain dropped down, and strengthened, and the gusts blew the rain into long lancing streamers into the faces of the crowds.

Someone I couldn't see in the crowd at my back and whose voice I did not know mumbled something about this being a day of ill omen.

I remained fast

In any great enterprise one has to contend with the faint-hearted. Not by dragging him down, but by reassuring his comrades he would one day achieve success.

All the same; this did in very truth seem to me to be a day of ill-omen.

What chilled me at the very thought of it was simple.

Somewhere out there, among those crowds taking part in the ceremonies of consecration, stood a man who was not a man, was more than a man, was a werewolf.

He would be standing there in a pious attitude, head bowed at appropriate moments, genuflecting, looking up at the open-air altars and the priests, taking part in the chanting and the prayers. What would he be thinking?

Contempt for us poor mortal fools?

Cunning plans to circumvent all our own plans?

Ravenous lust and hot desire at the prospect of his next girl-victim?

Or, just perhaps, a tinge of fear?

A tiny zephyr of apprehension when he looked about at the vast crowds, and saw the dudinter weapons?

No, no. Somehow I did not believe that our Ganchark of Vondium was frightened by all our fancy weapons and our chanting and mumbojumbo.

He remained locked into his belief in his own supernatural prowess.

That seemed certain to me as I stood and the rain belted down and we all got soaked.

That night after we'd all taken the Baths of the Nine and eaten hugely, we heard stories coming in from the countryside of all manner of evil portents. Horrid signs had been seen. The usual scad of two-headed animals was reported. Any stupid accident was magnified into a certain pointer to disaster.

Even the Headless Zorcamen had been seen.

Now this one annoyed me, for we'd already punctured that silly superstition. Yet, folk still believed, still thought that evil times brought out the Headless Zorcamen to ride across Vallia in dire warning . . .

Carrying a goblet of fine Gremivoh I wandered out onto the terrace. The stars were obscured. At my back through the pillared windows the sounds of the people enjoying themselves floated out onto the night air. At the moment I craved solitude; yet if good old Seg had walked out after me I'd have been pleased to see him. He saw me go out and without a smile turned back to talk to those in the group about him. He knew my ways a little by now, did Seg Segutorio, King of Croxdrin, Hyr-Kov elect.

A single thickish figure by the head of the flight of steps intrigued me. The figure seemed to writhe about and then parted. It split into two. I sauntered over.

Well, now!

If this kind of thing was going to carry on when the regiment of Jikai Vuvushis stood guard . . .!

I knew the guardsman, young Nafto the Hair. He was hairy, at that. He stood tall and straight, rigid. He licked his lip as I approached, and swallowed.

I did not know the girl, of course. She was just such a Battle Maiden as those I'd seen in fights, in skirmishes and ambushes. She wore the kit of a Sister of the Sword, her rapier at her side, and, also, she carried a light halberd. This was her sign of office, stating that she was a jurukker on guard duty.

Handling this trifling but pertinent incident could be tricky. A light touch seemed to me to be essential. A heavy-handed approach might work; I doubted it.

Anyway, when a fellow and a girl catch a monotonous night guard-duty together, well, nature is nature, propinquity will strike, a man is just a man and a woman is just a woman, and well . . .

I said, "Lahal, Nafto. How is the lady Nomee?"

In the lights of the torches his cheeks flared up. He looked furtive. He had every damn right to be furtive. I happened to know that he was betrothed to the lady Nomee.

"Lahal, majister. She is well, I thank you."

"Good." I turned to the Warrior Maiden. "Lahal, and your name is?"

"Lahal, majister." As she spoke I thought I caught an odd random gleam of the torches from her eyes. They sparkled brilliantly. Most odd. "I am Jinia ti Follendorf, and it please you. I am but recently returned from Hamal."

"You were with Stromni Marion?"

"Yes, majister. We were rescued just in time by the Jiktar and Strom Nango."

"I have heard the story. It was a brave deed, if sad."

"Yes, majister."

"Well, now, Jurukker Nafto. You are from 2ESW, and Jurukker Jinia ti Follendorf from the new detachment of Jikai Vuvushis has no doubt been entrusted to your care."

"That is so, majister. But my tour of duty is ended and I but wait for Larghos the Dome to relieve me." As he spoke we heard the quick step upon the flagstones. "And here he is now, majister."

I stepped back and let the guards get on with it. The Deldar changed guards very smartly when he saw me in the shadows. Yet that is an injustice. Deldar Fresk Ffanglion would do his duty smartly no matter when and where. Larghos the Dome took post. Nafto stepped across to fall in beside the Deldar. Just before he gave the order to march off, Fresk Ffanglion cocked a wary eye at me.

I nodded.

Vastly relieved, he marched off to the next guard post with his detail. Slowly, after a polite word to the new guard and to his companion, Jinia ti Follendorf, I sauntered down from the terrace and wandered off into the gardens.

Once the girls were in sufficient strength to form a full-size regiment, they would stand guard by themselves. All the same, there would be times in the future when men and women stood guard duty together.

Oh, well, nature was nature. If one interfered only worse complications could ensue, tragedy might follow.

The rain had ceased, washing the air to allow the sweet night scents to permeate everything. The moon blooms were particularly strong on a cloudless night, so that with the cloud cover above all the other scents so often overlooked could be savored on this night.

Again I gave no particular thought to the way of it. A footfall on the gravel at my back was not the quiet tread of the guards. It was, also, not Seg's usual light hunting step. I turned easily, to see Seg walking up and deliberately making all this noise for my benefit.

"Hai, Seg!" I said at once, letting him know he was welcome. Well, hell's bells and buckets of blood! There are precious few times when Seg is not welcome.

"You prosper, my old dom?"

"Hardly." I told him about two jurukkers kissing each other on guard duty.

He guffawed.

"These youngsters don't know how good they've got it, by the Veiled Froyvil!"

"When we get up to Turko and start knocking seven kinds of brickdust out of Layco Jhansi they'll have no time for amorous combat. Believe me."

"Oh, aye!"

We saw the white flitting figure of a girl running between the flowerbeds, a moth in that erratic light.

As I say, again I gave no particular thought to the way of it.

Seg started forward.

"The foolish girl . . ."

What she was about we could only conjecture. We started at a run after her.

The hoarse snarling growls, the desperate screams, the horrid guttural sounds of bestial triumph drove us on in a lung-bursting run.

CHAPTER TWELVE

"THE DRATTED THING'S DEAD ALL RIGHT."

Together we burst out beyond the edge of the shrubbery and stared across an open flower bed area. The blood thumped around my body and I could feel my heart going nineteen to the dozen. The feel of the sword in my fist gave me some reassurance—some, by Krun, only some!

The werewolf appeared huge, menacing. The girl lay upon the path, sprawled, her white dress glimmering in that mothlike appearance in the random illumination.

As we raced up, the ganchark lifted his head. The muzzle gaped, sharp fangs yellow within the darkness. His eyes in that wolfish fashion burned red.

Seg skidded to a halt. His bow was in his fist.

Seg Segutorio, least of any Bowman of Loh, was not going to walk around in our present position without his famed Lohvian longbow. He drew, lifted, loosed in that lightning fast reflex that dazzles the eye.

Bending, I hurled myself forward under the shaft and to the side, keeping out of Seg's line of sight.

Before I reached the werewolf and the girl three arrows sprouted from the thing's breast.

It screeched hideously, pawing unavailingly at the shafts.

Then I was on it.

The dudinter blade smeared with ganjid slid into his belly. The blade ripped up, twisting brutally, tearing, bursting the thing's heart.

It screamed and fell.

It fell on the girl.

I gave it a vicious kick, toppling it over on its side. The girl's eyes were closed, there was blood on her skin through a long rent in the dress; but she still breathed.

Seg was with me.

We were both panting as though we'd run an enormous distance instead of the less than a hundred paces from the point where we'd first spotted the werewolf. Seg kicked the gray carcass. The hair hung lank and twisted, the vicious head lolled, the muzzle gaping, the tongue curled between those yellow fangs.

"We've done it!" said Seg. He whooped a breath. "May Erthyr be praised!"

"Aye," I said. "By Zim-Zair, I really believe the thing is dead."

"Oh, aye, my old dom. The dratted thing's dead all right."

In a hollering rush we were surrounded by guards. High-held torchlights illuminated the scene. The pooled blood shone crimson. I ripped out an intemperate order.

"Run for the needleman! Run for a puncture lady! The girl is sore hurt."

More than one person ran off, and this pleased me.

We all stood in a ring with the torches streaming their orange hair above us. The light showed up every detail.

Some of us gasped. One or two screamed. Others

cursed deep in their throats. Most of us, I was glad
to see, stood looking stonily on.

The werewolf changed.

The evil metamorphosis that had gripped him slack-
ened its hold now he was dead, loosening the bonds
that chained him to the wolf form. The lank gray hair
rippled and curled away. The hideous fanged muzzle shimmered as it changed, turning back into a
man's mouth and chin. The ears rounded and flattened.
The whole form flowed and melted as a child's choco-
late doll melts in the sunshine upon the windowsill.

But, instead of sloughing away into a puddled mess,
the ganchark took on another form—its true form.

We stood looking down upon the body of a young
man.

Now the people gasped again, and this time there
were more oaths, more curses in that crowd.

We stood looking down upon the dead body of
Jurukker Nafto the Hair.

Oddly enough, in that moment, the clouds directly
above us parted in a waft of an unfelt breeze. The
light of the Maiden with the Many Smiles broke
through, shedding a pink radiance down. In that
moment the petals of the moon-blooms opened. On a
sudden the air was filled with the scents of moonblooms, strikingly pungent in the night

A stout, high-colored, buxom woman pushed
through the throng, swinging her bag so that it struck
shrewdly against shins in an impartial way as she
cleared a path for herself. She wore a tromp-colored
dress with a high collar. She glanced at poor dead
Nafto the Hair, sniffed, and bent to the girl.

This formidable puncture lady was Prishilla the
Otlora—Otlora being translated means something like
No-nonsense.

"She'll live," she said, her voice oddly and affectionately gruff. "Now give me some room to work."

That seemed to break the spell.

Garfon the Staff could take charge. He'd handle all the ugly necessaries that, for a dizzy moment, seemed quite beyond me, emperor or no damned emperor.

Seg gave me a nudge.

"Brassud, my old dom. It's all over. Let's go and find a wet."

"Aye, You're right. Although—there will have to be an inquiry."

"Of course. Let's get out of this."

The people already on the scene hung about, and more folk running up crowded in. The place was congested, excitement rippled in the night air like lightning. I made no attempt to halt any of this. Let the people see. Let it be known that the famed and feared Ganchark of Vondium had been trapped and slain.

Bad cess to the dratted thing!

A guard appeared holding high bits of a jurukker's kit. They had been found bundled behind a bush. No doubt Nafto would have returned for them later. Well, he'd never don the kit of an imperial jurukker, ever again proudly wear the emperor's insignia. He was no longer of 2ESW.

He had been a werewolf.

And now he was dead.

"D'you think they'll have him down in the Ice Floes of Sicce?"

I considered the thought as Seg led off toward the terrace.

"I don't see why not. He is, after all, a human being now, and he's dead. No doubt he'll trot around the Ice Floes for a space, meet the Gray Ones, before he—"

"Oh, I don't know about that," said Seg. "D'you think he'll ever get up to the sunny uplands beyond?"

"I really don't know. I can't find it in my heart to hate the poor devil. We've got to find out *why* he turned into a ganchark."

"I don't believe anyone ever has."

"A great load has been lifted. A black cloud has passed away from Vondium. We'll have to have a tremendous celebration and thanksgiving service. The priests will do us proud. And there's Deb-Lu."

"Thank Opaz."

An old, a very old little ditty, popped into my mind as we went across the terrace and through the corridors to our private snug.

> "March winds and April showers,
> Bring forth May flowers."

Well, Zair knew, the seasons on Kregen are markedly different from those on Earth. The idea was that we'd gone through the rain and the winds, now we could look forward to a time of blooming. That was the hope.

Ha!

Kregen—ah, Kregen! The world is wild and terrifying, and beautiful and enjoyable. Much goes on there that is just simply unbelievable by Earthly standards. And, also, because men are men and women are women, much goes on there that anyone on this Earth would instantly recognize. Beauty and terror go hand in hand, it seems . . .

In the way of things on Kregen, the little meeting of Seg, and Nath na Kochwold, and Farris and me broadened and grew, and we moved to a larger chamber where the tables were well provisioned with wine and delicacies. We might be up all night talking and arguing, going over and over what had occurred, pondering, wondering, planning for the future. These night-time gatherings were among the more important of periods for me, as you know, wherein much was decided that would directly affect the fate of Vallia, of Paz, and of Kregen itself. Not, of course, to mention the effect those decisions would have upon Delia and me . . .

The upshot of one of those decisions was that directly after the thanksgiving service the force destined for Turko would fly off. Seg and I would go. Now that the werewolf was slain, there was nothing detaining us in the capital. Farris could handle everything with the Presidio, as he and they had been doing so splendidly.

As well as being the emperor's Justicar Crebent, Farris was also the Lord Supremo of the Vallian Air Service.

"I can spare you ample vollers and vorlcas for the whole force, Dray. But let me have 'em back as soon as you can."

He didn't have to tell me why he wanted the airboats and the flying sailing ships of the sky back so promptly. We in Vondium had to be prepared to send forces anywhere at a moment's notice to resist invasion. We were that blind man at the center, striking out at invisible foes who attacked him from all sides.

"Thank you, Farris. Done."

Nath na Kochwold eased over. He looked just a little flushed and this was not from wine but from a nervous effort he was making. I guessed instantly what was afoot.

"Now, majis, the position is this. You are taking the Sixth Kerchuri with you to strengthen Kov Turko, who has the whole of the Fourth Phalanx. That will give him three full Kerchuris. Now, then—"

Mildly, I cut in to say, "Did you not say that this new green Fifth Phalanx you have formed needs your personal ministrations, Nath?"

"Well, I may have made that statement at one time." He gestured widely. "Of course, that might have been true. But they are not really green troops, as you well know. And they have first-class instructors. No, no. They will improve without me. But, the position of three full Kerchuris in the field, I submit, majis, does demand the personal attention of—"

"Of a Kapt of the Phalanx?"

He coughed. "You have done me the honor to name me Krell-Kapt of the Phalanx. I really do think—"

"Well, let me think on it."

Then Seg butted in, in his shrewd yet fey way.

"Three Kerchuris demand a Krell-Kapt, Dray. I think Turko, and his general, Kapt Erndor, have been controlling the Ninth Army up there excellently. But with these reinforcements . . ."

I said, "Any high-ranking chuktar can take command of an army and be named its Kapt. When the army's campaigns are over, the chuktar relinquishes his title of Kapt. That is simple."

"But the Phalanx is different. Nath is the Krell-Kapt of the entire Phalanx Force. They will hardly ever serve together. So the Brumbytevaxes take command of each individual phalanx, and, as we all know, the Kerchurivaxes with their kerchuris do the work. So—"

"I think, Seg, you have put your boot into your

own argument. If the Kervaxes do all the work, and the Brumbytevaxes are an unnecessary luxury, there is even less need for a superior over them."

Nath took a cautious sip of his wine, did not look at me, did not look at Seg. I could see he was suffering.

The name of Brumbytevax had been given as a kind of nickname, a totem-name, to the commanders of each phalanx. It was true the Kerchurivaxes handled most of the work. And the very name of the pikemen in the files, the brumbytes, given to the commander of the whole phalanx, was in very truth a form of affectionate recognition of their position. On the other hand, the phalanx commanders had been in tough fights, when the phalanx fought as a whole, some pretty fraught encounters, too . . .

I said, "Brytevax Dekor might very well expect to command the Sixth Kerchuri when it arrives up with his Fourth Phalanx."

"Aye, majis, aye," groaned Nath. "That's the rub."

Fixing Nath na Kochwold—who is a man very strict on discipline—with a stern eye, I ground out: "Can you personally assure me that the Fifth Phalanx will be trained up properly in your absence?"

He stiffened. The wine-goblet drooped at his side. It was empty. He rapped out his words as though on parade.

"Aye, majister! I so assure you, as Opaz is my witness."

"Right. That's good enough for me. Thank Seg. In his cunning way of Erthyrdrin he's twisted all logic inside out. Nath, you'll come with us."

"Thank you, majister."

I turned away to find a refill, thinking what a lot of rigmarole went on when grown men wanted to go marching off to war. Give me half a chance and I'd stay at home and let some other idiot get on with the fighting and the killing. But, then, I had been landed with this job of being Emperor of Vallia, and so I had a duty to go and do what I could for the place . . .

The foolishness of a girl's heart was discussed, and its near-tragic end marveled at. Nafto the Hair had been something of a romancer. Well, kissing a girl whilst on guard duty was heinous enough. He had been betrothed to the lady Nomee. Yet he'd made an assignation with a young girl from the palace household—a newcomer I didn't recognize—and must have been persuasive enough to cause her to forget the werewolf. She had been warned not to go out alone at night. Yet she'd flitted off to keep her assignation, no doubt trembling with fears that had nothing to do with gancharks.

Poor Filti the Sheets was now abed, nastily cut-up by claws but otherwise physically unharmed. As I had conjectured concerning Wenerl the Lightfoot, so I wondered if Filti's mind would fully recover from her ordeal.

Deb-Lu-Quienyin looked in briefly on his way to bed. He appeared tired; but his indomitable will overcame effects of age without sorcerous aids.

We discussed what had occurred for a time, and then Deb-Lu said:

"Jak, I must comment on peculiar phenomena recently observed by me in the environs of the palace."

"Phenomena?"

"Precisely. Not, I need scarcely add, on the physical plane."

"Scarcely."

This renowned Wizard of Loh and I had passed through some harum-scarum and some frightening experiences together. He had known me as Jak. Now and again he could bring himself to call me Dray, and in general company would use the familiar term majis. But, as with a number of other people, I remained Jak for him

"The necessity to delve back into my childhood and recall methods of dealing with werewolves, and of the formula—Emder, the dear fellow, called it my magical recipe—for the ganjid potion, distracted me considerably. Some occult force has been up to something, yet I cannot tell what that may be, for the visitations are brief."

"It's not another wizard gone into lupu and spying on us?"

"I think not. There is probably an element of spying involved. Vallia has enemies abroad. But after the death of Phu-Si-Yantong, well, one could hope we had seen the last of evil wizards."

I essayed a smile at my comrade wizard.

"On Kregen, Deb-Lu? Not to be troubled by any more evil wizards or witches? Come now, old friend, you have more faith in the inevitable than that!"

CHAPTER THIRTEEN

WE FLY TO
TURKO'S FALINUR

My decision to fly north to Falinur aboard a vorlca, one of Vallia's sailing ships of the clouds, caused a deal of quiddities, I know, and must have seemed odd. Also, I suspect, there were a few folk who felt quite put out by that decision.

To fly aboard a voller, one of the airboats that had the ability not only to lift themselves into the air but to speed along at a good clip, was a much sought after treat. Vollers were still scarce. The two silver boxes, one containing a mix of minerals, the other cayferm, which lifted airboats, remained difficult to manufacture after the depredations in Hamal where most of them still originated. We in Vallia could make silver boxes that would lift a ship into the air and cling onto the lines of ethero-magnetic force. Thus the ship could put a keel, as it were, out and, hoisting sail, tack and make boards against the wind.

You can easily, therefore, see why I chose to go aboard a sailing flier. For a salty old sea-dog like me, although the scent of the sea might be absent, there was the breeze in the canvas, the creak of timber, the feel of a ship alive and vibrant all about me.

One day—and soon we all hoped—we would produce our own silver boxes to power vollers. I heaved up a sigh.

"What ails you, then, my old dom?" called a familiar voice.

"I was thinking of Jaezila and Tyfar."

Seg turned to look forward. We stood right in the eyes of the ship. Massy clouds soared above us as we soared over the green landscape below. Every shred of canvas was set and pulling, stiff as boards. This vessel, *Logan's Fancy*, might not be the largest sailer of the skies we had built; she was truly among the fastest.

"That Prince Tyfar needs to have his head careened and his brains scraped." Seg spoke seriously, and I did not miss the almost savage note behind his words. He had been in loco parentis to Jaezila during my enforced imprisonment on Earth. "By Vox! I wonder what mischief they're up to over in the Mountains of the West."

"If they can keep the wildmen at bay and ensure supplies for the silver boxes, then whatever else they get up to is their own business."

"Well, the quicker they decide, the better. Milsi wants to meet them, for a start."

"Your Milsi, Seg, is a jewel."

"Oh, aye."

"And I could wish she and Delia were with us."

"We'll just have to bash Layco Jhansi and see Turko right, then we can get back to Vondium. No doubt by that time their business with the Sisters of the Rose will be over."

"One can only live in pious hope. Ah, here comes Deb-Lu. There are things you and he must know."

"Lahal, Jak—what are these things, then?"

The breeze whispered past as we were carried along in its warm embrace. Zim and Genodras flooded down the streaming mingled lights of the Suns of

Scorpio. The day was good. Yet I had information to tell these two that would cast a dark blot upon their appreciation of that bright scene.

A flurried commotion aft did not make us turn our heads. Back there a series of stout poles protruded from the side of the ship. These were the perching poles for the squadron of flutduins we carried, and these birds are, as I have often said and will no doubt say again, the best saddle birds of all Paz—in my estimation. Their flyers were lads and girls trained up by my Djangs, for Vallia had been lagging far behind other countries when it came to the use of aerial forces of animal and bird flyers.

The birds would swoop in splendidly from either side, give a neat little flick of their broad wings, do a sideslip and so land on their selected perching pole. Strong curved claws would grasp the timber. The riders would unstrap their clerketers and use the nets strung beneath to reach the bulwarks. When I looked at these perching poles bearing their aerial freight I was reminded of an abacus.

"Turko will be pleased to see those," remarked Seg.

"And these things, Jak?"

"Well now, Deb-Lu. I told you we were unlikely to be left unmolested by wizards and witches on Kregen. I've told Seg a little of what we met in the Coup Blag in the Snarly Hills away down south in Pandahem. Our ways parted then, Milsi and Seg sorted out her realm, I did what I could against the perverted followers of Lem the Silver Leem, and also against the armies being formed in North Pandahem to attack us in southwest Vallia."

"I suspect You Bear No Good Tidings."

"Yes. Phu-Si-Yantong might be dead; his shadow still hovers over us."

"Ah! I had heard rumors of a child . . ." There was no need for Deb-Lu to elaborate on the ways in which wizards circulated their news. He wouldn't tell me, anyway. But they kept up with what went on in their uncanny fashions.

"The Child is an uhu. A hermaphrodite, called Phunik. He has great powers already, although not yet grown into his strength. He is very much an unknown factor."

Deb-Lu looked surprised. He gave that ridiculous turban a shove. "You mean the danger comes from the child's mother?"

"Yes."

Seg said: "She'll be a Witch of Loh, for sure."

"Of course." Deb-Lu rubbed his nose. "This is amazing news. I was firmly under the apprehension that Ling-Li-Lwingling was dead."

Now it was my turn to be surprised. Surprised! By Krun, I felt the shock go through me.

"Ling-Li-Lwingling!" I yelped. "Oh, no, San, not her. The witch is Csitra—"

Seg put out a hand and caught Deb-Lu as he stumbled. If he would have fallen I do not know. If the news had shaken him into an incautious movement, if he felt dazed, I did not know. But he looked up at me with eyes that reflected a greater shadow than that which I thought I was telling him about . . .

"Csitra," he whispered.

"She queens it over her maze in the Coup Blag and terrorizes the whole district. I was extremely fortunate to escape from her clutches."

The Star Lords may or may not have assisted me in that fraught escape. Powerful though a wizard or witch might be, and supremely powerful though the Witches and Wizards of Loh truly are, yet their arcane knowledge pales to insignificancee beside the awesome powers of the Star Lords.

For some weird reason the memory of one of the stories circulating in Vondium added significance to what we were saying. Covell of the Golden Tongue, young still and virile, a master poet, had spent months composing a stunning verse epic. This was duly staged, presented, put on, in Ramon's Club theater, which, belying its name, held seating for upwards of a thousand people on one level alone.

Covell of the Golden Tongue was shattered.

Ramon had emasculated the epic, shortened it, left out the ending, rendered the whole grotesque. I had only heard this story and could not vouch for its truth. What I did realize was that Deb-Lu's reactions at the name of the Witch of Loh, Csitra, indicated that we might plan out how events were to shape, and someone else—the Witch Csitra—would devise a new and horrible ending . . .

Around us in thin air the flying ships and the airboats of this little force sailed majestically on. Against the forces of sorcery we, ourselves, were puny indeed.

Seg half-turned.

"A glass of strong red for the San!" he bellowed. One of the youngsters, smart in his new uniform, sprang up and bolted aft. In only moments the glass of wine was to hand. Deb-Lu took it and drank gratefully.

"Ling-Li-Lwingling," I said. "She *was* mixed up with that devil Phu-Si-Yantong, then, after all." And, I confess it, I didn't much care for the note of uneasiness in my voice, didn't care one little bit, by Vox!

"Only insofar, from your news about Csitra, Jak, that she was able to elude him. Perhaps, she is not dead. I sincerely hope so, for there was much good in her."

I'd first made the acquaintance, passing, with scant ceremony, of the Witch of Loh Ling-Li-Lwingling down south in Jikaida City in the Dawn Lands of Havilfar. That was no long time after Deb-Lu-Quienyin and I had first met. At that time he'd no idea of the schemes dominating the crazed mind of Phu-Si-Yantong. Now I said:

"She blames us for the death of her wizard. Her uhu, Phunik, hates us all. There is no doubt that between them they mean to continue with Phu-Si-Yantong's insane plans."

A silence fell between us filled with the creak of timber and the whisper of the breeze, the flutterings of the flutduins and the busy work of the ship about us. Gray and white clouds ahead indicated we might have to think about a course change soon. All that fascinating aerial navigation and ship-handling could be left to the captains and their officers. More and more I found these good folk who knew their tasks a trifle reticent when I wandered in to lend a hand. This was understandable; but I regretted the passing of that phase of my career as an emperor.

Seg at last said: "When we were escaping from the Coup Blag and making our way through that dratted jungle in Pandahem, we had a visitation. A phantom in a golden throne appeared in midair. We took that to be Csitra spying on us."

Sharply, I said: "And Deb-Lu, you are confident she has not been spying on us here?"

In answer the wizard began with circumlocution.

"We Wizards and Witches of Loh keep our secrets close, as we must. I can tell you a little, for I know that there has seldom, if ever, been a relationship between Lohvian Sorcerers and non-Lohvian Sorcerers as exists between us." He did not push his turban straight, although it toppled dangerously over his ear. "Phu-Si-Yantong and I studied together. We were not too close. There were others we held in greater esteem. But he and I were on a par."

A shout from the foretop took my attention over the bows. A tiny black dot showed ahead skipping between the clouds. As Deb-Lu continued to speak I watched that distant speck.

"I do know that Yantong desperately desired Ling-Li-Lwingling, and that she, considerably younger, wanted nothing of him. Our codes—well, I can say that he could not force her with thaumaturgy for the punishment that would fall on him. The witch, Csitra, desired Yantong and remained faithful to him throughout—and her powers were mirrored in his."

I said: "I believe her to be a woman who remains faithful to one man."

Deb-Lu nodded. The turban swayed. "That is true."

"Then I breathe a little easier."

Seg's voice reached me over my shoulder, for he stood a little to the rear and side and he, too, I guessed, was watching that approaching dot in the distance.

"Oh, my old dom? That sounds highly mysterious."

I did not laugh lightly, although, in all truth, the situation could have called for an affected reaction of that kind.

"In all the horror and the maze of the Coup Blag Csitra pretended to be Queen Mab—"

"She what!" exploded Seg.

"I was taken in for a space. Then, when she made perfectly plain that her advances were strengthened by witchcraft, and I came to my senses, and escaped—"

Seg did not quite guffaw; but infectious amusement bubbled in his words. "She took a shine to you! She fancies you! Oh, oh, my old dom, you've a lot to answer for when certain people gather around . . ."

Well, I still believed passionately that I'd done enough to escape the clutches of Cistra through my own belief in Delia. The Star Lords had given me a breathing space in which to make good my escape. But Seg was right. Csitra had prevented her child, Phunik, from torturing me to death. I still believed she would not allow that. So we had a time in which to fight back.

Yantong had thought to use me, and so had ordered his human tools not to have me assassinated; now Csitra gave the same orders through her misguided passion.

It was, as you will readily perceive, ironic. All I was concerned with was staying alive until my work in Vallia and Paz was completed.

The speck flitting between the clouds broadened and grew, sprouted wings, glittered with harness, turned into a wide-pinioned flutduin breasting the air in a long slanting descent to our leading ship.

"That'll be a messenger from Turko welcoming us in."

"Aye," I said. "And I hope he brings news of better weather. We'll have to circle around those clouds, I think."

Deb-Lu at last lifted a hand and pushed his turban straight. "I shall continue to make observations to discover what these swift flashes of thaumaturgical art may be. I'll have a word with Khe-Hi. He may be experiencing the same effects with Prince Drak in the southwest."

The incoming flyer made a straight line for *Logan's Fancy*. Superb birds, flutduins, masters of the air. The rider sat hunched and I caught no glimpse of weaponry jutting arrogantly upwards, streaming his colors.

With a single half-circle to bring him around and match speeds, the flutduin rippled those powerful wings, his claws extended and he was down, gripping to a perching pole. Seg and I walked aft to greet the messenger. When we reached the cleared space of deck paralleling the line of perching poles we could see that all was not as it should be.

Four crewmen were out on the nets, balancing, bringing the flyer in. His arms and legs dangled. Those arms under the flying leathers would be banded with sleeves of ocher and umber checks, lined-out in red. Those were the colors of Falinur, the schturval of Kov Turko.

The Ship-Deldar, Bolto the Knot, looked up from the bulwarks where he'd been yelling at his men. As the Bosun, he had, perforce, to possess a pair of lungs. His hard and lumpy face reminded me of the time he'd taken those lumps fighting at my side.

"He's sore hurt, majister. I've sent for the needleman; but there seems little chance for the poor fambly."

We watched as the men brought the messenger inboard and placed him down on hastily piled cloaks. He looked ghastly, and an arrow stood between his ribs. The feathers of that shaft were a hard bright blue.

At this, Seg's face tautened.

The messenger was a Brokelsh, his hair coarse and his ways, no doubt, uncouth; yet he was a man and he was dying. He tried to speak, and blood frothed his lips.

"Kov Turko sends . . . urgent . . . meetingplace . . . hurry—"

His head lolled, his eyelids closed, and he was dead.

Dolan the Pills, the needleman, stood back and shook his head.

"There is nothing I can do for him, poor fellow."

We stood there grouped about the dead man. He had given his life to serve Vallia, yet we did not know in what fraught action he had died. There was no need for me to do or say anything regarding the proprieties. The sailors of Vallia know how to respect their dead.

Presently, when we'd gone into the cabin to drink a small private toast, Captain Nath Hardolf came in to say that in his opinion the change of course would have to be made within the next glass. The clouds ahead looked more ugly by the moment . . .

"Well, now, Captain Nath," I said, lowering the glass. "Let us have the charts out."

He gave me a puzzled look; but the charts of the land ahead were brought in. We bent over them spread upon the table, the glasses and bottles pushed to the side.

"Here," I said, and stabbed a forefinger down, "is where we agreed to meet Kov Turko."

Captain Nath Hardolf could see, all right.

He was representative of those master sailing captains of Vallia, seasoned, experienced, long in the tooth. He had had his share of tragedies and triumphs in life, and command of *Logan's Fancy* was perhaps not with him the pinnacle of his career it would have been to a less-experienced master mariner.

The point where we had agreed to meet up with Turko's wing of the army he commanded here lay directly beyond the storm. The gale could broom us all away, could blow us to Hell and Kingdom Come. If we tacked around the gale we would take so much longer that whatever the urgency that had given that poor dead messenger his quietus would never receive any help from us. By the time we arrived up Turko and his army could have been destroyed.

"Very good, majister," said Captain Hardolf. "I'll see everything is battened down."

"Excellent. Pass on the message to the rest of the fleet. We are going straight through that damned storm up ahead, and gale or no gale, it won't stop us from reaching Kov Turko in time."

CHAPTER FOURTEEN

THE BATTLE OF MARNDOR

An armada of sails coursing through thin air . . . The streaming mingled lights of the Suns of Scorpio sheening from straining canvas . . . The sparkling glitter striking back from gilding and gingerbread, from ornate high-flung sterns and towers, from shooting galleries and menacing boarding platforms . . . Oh, yes, the sailing ships of the skies of Kregen provide a spectacle dazzling and inspiring. Silently above the land they soar, the wind of their passage lost and blown away in the breeze.

And I, Dray Prescot, Lord of Strombor and Krozair of Zy, calmly gave orders that would hurl all that mighty armada between the jaws of destruction ahead.

For, make no mistake about it, just because I said the gale would not prevent us from joining up with Turko's army did not mean we would. Oh, no! My bravado could toss all away in ruination . . .

There is a saying common in the seas of Paz that a smart vessel is 'All shipshape and Vallian fashion.'

In the moments before we plunged into black danger those aerial sailors of Vallia proved the saying true.

The vollers with their command of forward motion took the vorlcas in tow, for the latter's sails would be

of no help, would be a positive hindrance in the fight
ahead. Tow ropes were passed, the wires made fast.
In a sighing flutter of multi-colored collapse, all the
canvas came in. There was time for some of the
vessels who possessed them to strike their topmasts.
We battened down.

The flutduins were brought in off their perching
poles. The magnificent birds sensed the foul weather
ahead, and made only a few formal protests at being
cooped up. A wing beat, the wide gape of a beak,
and then they settled down. The poles were run in
and lashed down.

All this was repeated in all the vessels, signals
flickering like summer lightning from mast to mast.

"We're ready, majister." Captain Nath Hardolf
stumped up to make his report.

"Excellent, Cap'n Nath. Now, by Vox, we shall
see!"

"By Corg, majister! I think I shall enjoy this day.
It will be something to make the blood run more
freely in my veins."

I eyed him. Yes, his professionalism and experience were of such an order that little excited him in
these latter days of command. Well, now, he was
being handed a little excitement. One is never too
old to learn, never too old to love, never too old to
taste of life . . .

In his daily life and with his usual professional
caution, Captain Hardolf had probably never been
anywhere near a storm for years . . .

The gale would refresh him, test him, and play
havoc with the fleet. Battened down, all made fast,
we coursed on through the air toward those frowning
pinnacles of cloud. The blackness rose up before us
and the lights of day faded and muted to a wan

ghostly underwater luminosity, which rapidly sloughed away into blackness.

The gale took us in its jaws and shook us. The wind shrieked and howled and scourged us. We forged on.

Well, well . . . There are gales in life, and we weather them or we do not. Like a broken quarry in the fangs of a leem, we struggled feebly and resisted as best we could. This gale did what it had to do to us, and we took our punishment, and we did not give up the fight, and at last, we broke through into the streaming lights of Zim and Genodras beyond . . .

A goodly proportion of the folk aboard wore green faces . . .

Only two tows parted. The shipwrights of Vallia build well and only one vessel was shattered and broken into pieces and so fell all that awful distance to the ground with her people spilling out like dust shaken from a broom.

Not everyone had been issued with a belt containing its two small silver boxes which would keep a person drifting gently to the ground. Not all. We in Vallia built what we could with the resources we had. These horrors are the price of empire. Once more I knew that I was racing past the point at which I could no longer face the spiritual agony of paying that price.

"We have done well, majister." Captain Hardolf's face held a flush along the cheekbones. He looked sprightly. "Now I believe Corg does sometimes smile on us."

The ship that had foundered, *Naghan's Reply*, had been one of the older vessels of the force, containing spearmen. The loss was regrettable, but I felt thanks that we had not lost any brumbytes, or archers, or heavy infantry. Of cavalry we were short—as usual. The flutduin aerial force was going to have to perform prodigiously.

Seg had taken the blue-fletched arrow embedded in the body of Turko's messenger and he studied it intently. I understood his unease and shared it. At least, we did have a splendid regiment of my own Valkan Archers with us.

Marion's Jikai Vuvushis kept in good heart—nor was there any reason to suspect they would not. My own crusty kampeons in the guard corps took everything in their stride, phlegmatically, cursingly, explosively, according to their natures.

So we soared out into the radiance of the twin suns, spewed out like pips from an orange. We were still battened down. We were battered. Some malignant fringes of the gale threw a last cavort of wind at us, tumbling us about. Spread out below us across the plain lay the tents and encampments of an army.

This army had been harassed by the storm, for many tents had been blown down, animal lines broken and we could almost muster smiles at the antics of the folk down there, chasing over the plain after the stampeding animals.

"Plenty of space to let down," observed Captain Hardolf. "We shall not be troubled by trees, I fancy."

"The quicker we are down and can set ourselves to rights, the better." Seg's voice, as sure and calm as ever, reassured me in an odd way. I felt edgy. Well, by Zim-Zair, didn't a fellow have every right to feel off-color and snappy when through his own orders other good men and women went in peril of their lives?

Our appearance caused an immediate stir in the camp below. As we lowered through the air the pale blobs of faces turned up, we could see people running, and many of those off chasing runaway animals started back for the camp.

"Turko has a sizable force here," observed Nath na Kochwold. He leant over the rail, shading his eyes.

"What the hell was his hurry?" demanded Seg.

The first ships touched the ground. Crewmen sprang out to make all secure. When I went over the side I knew there would be a great gang of hulking lads to surround me. And, now, there would be the lithe forms of Jikai Vuvushis among that formidable guard. . . .

The breeze in the aftermath of the gale still blew briskly; the air held that fresh minty tang and the grass glittered with millions of spearpoints of light. One after the other the vessels touched down. We took up a neat and prescribed pattern for landing. A damned great voller came down in front of *Logan's Fancy* and obscured my view of the camp.

"Well, Turko'll be rushing across here as fast as he can," I said. "We'd better go down to meet him."

"I'm looking forward to seeing that man again," said Seg, and he rubbed his hands.

"If you want to try a fall or three with him, Seg—"

"What!" He laughed. "I'd as lief try to wrestle a mountain out of the ground, or a river from its bed."

"Very poetic." A very great Khamorro, a master of the martial arts, Turko. His bare hands were far more lethal than many a weapon in other less-skilled hands.

Afterwards, we tried to work out who had yelled first. No one could say who it was who first raised the alarm. All we did know was that in one moment we were thankful to be down and out of the gale, disembarking to greet friends, and in the next we were facing foemen viciously determined to destroy us all.

"The colors!" The yells racketed up. "Those are not the colors of Falinur! That's Vennar!"

And so it was.

Instead of Turko's banners of ocher and umber checks lined out in red, with the dragon as a dramatic symbol overhead, we could make out the colors of Vennar, ocher and silver, with the strigicaw as the symbol.

"Layco Jhansi!" I said. I felt like spitting. "Now we know what Turko's messenger died trying to tell us!"

Yes, we were caught by surprise. The ranks of Jhansi's men formed as they ran up from their camp. They were smart. The man who had been the old emperor's chief pallan, who had run his empire for him, who had conspired and tried to murder the emperor, whose treason had borne bitter fruit, was no man to employ mercenaries who were not top class.

In all the hullabaloo and rushing about, the lads of the guard corps showed that they, too, were not men to be flurried over falling into a trap. Even if, as evidently was the case, this was an unpremeditated trap.

In the nature of the composition of the guard corps the natural rivalry between the Emperor's Sword Watch and the Emperor's Yellow Jackets impelled mutual speed; by Bongolin! To see the lads whipping on their armor, latching all fast, clapping on their helmets, grabbing their weapons! They were rough, toughy, hairy fellows, and I echoed Old Beaky himself when I say that they might not impress the enemy, but, by Zair, they impressed me.

While all this went on I leaped for the ratlines of

the mainmast and went up as though I was back in a seventy-four in Nelson's Navy. Up and up to the cross-trees and there I could swivel and take a good look at the wasps' nest we had stirred up by falling into it.

There were a lot of them. This was a sizable force, twice ours, I estimated. I looked for the archers. That blue-fletched arrow through Turko's messenger told me what I would see, and I did.

Bowmen of Loh.

There they were, running to form their shooting blocks. Tall, redheaded men, and each with a great Lohvian longbow and a quiver of the shafts fletched with the feathers of the king korf, they were the most renowned of the archers of Paz. Layco Jhansi's pact with the Racters served him well, for hiring mercenaries of this quality took more than mere money. They demanded certain guarantees before they hired on. Jhansi had clearly given those guarantees; the right to plunder after the victories was only one.

A rapid survey of the situation convinced me that we could win the coming fight if we acted decisively and rapidly. I shinned down to the deck and yelled for Captain Hardolf.

"Majister?"

"Signal the fleet. We are taking off."

"Do what?" yelped Seg.

"Majister!" bellowed Nath na Kochwold. "My lads are disembarking now, ready for the fight—"

"Your Kerchuri will be shot to pieces, Nath."

"My chodku and your Valkan Archers will afford cover—"

"We can't run away," said Seg. "Turko—"

"Turko arranged to meet us here, on the Plain of Marndor, and sent a messenger to tell us to hurry somewhere else. Clearly, he has been driven back."

"In that case we blatter this lot and so relieve him."

The devil of it was, Seg was right. I was growing faint-hearted in these latter days, me, Dray Prescot. Yet the thought of sending this force of fine lads and girls to fight and die repelled me.

In any event, our hands were forced; for Jhansi's men simply put in a thundering great cavalry charge straight at us. Clearly, they hoped to topple us in this first onslaught and so win outright.

Rushing out from the ships and forming up as we were, Jhansi could do it. He could hit us before we were formed.

"Get some vollers aloft!" I bellowed. "Attack from the air. Break out the flutduins! *Bratch*!"

I grabbed Nath na Kochwold. I actually gripped his arm.

"Nath! Keep your Kerchuri close. Shields well up. We'll put you in when their first onslaught is blunted."

"But—"

"Do it!"

"Quidang!"

Targon the Tapster and Naghan ti Lodkwara came up to report 1ESW formed and ready to go and get stuck in—as they phrased it.

I said, "Good. You may have to bear the brunt at the beginning."

"As will we, majister!" roared Clardo the Clis, scarred, plug-ugly, his yellow uniform brilliant.

"Aye, majister," agreed Drill the Eye in his fiery way, squat and with a bowman's shoulders, his yellow uniform a match for Clardo's.

Clardo the Clis commanded the churgurs and Drill the Eye the archers of the First Regiment of the

Emperor's Yellow Jackets. They were not to be out-
done by their comradely rivals of IESW.

Fakal the Oivon, swarthy, was with them, a little
in the background as ever. Larghos the Sko-handed,
that long-featured hyrpaktun from Gremivoh, was
not with us, having gone to command the staff-slingers
of 3EYJ.

Marion stepped up, scarlet, ready to burst out
with Zair knew what kinds of rhetorical promises.

Quickly, I said, "Marion, I want your girls near me
in this fight. See to it."

She jumped, lost some of her color, said: "Quidang!"

Targon leered a laugh. "I'm not too happy about
leaving you with a bunch of lassies—"

Marion, again, started to speak, and Seg butted in.

"I'll take the Valkan Archers and play on 'em a bit,
warm 'em up. Mind you hit 'em good!"

"Oh, aye!"

· The way everyone wanted to interpose their bodies between me and the incoming shafts, the charging lance!

"This should prove interesting, Seg. I trust you'll
show these Bowmen of Loh what shafts fletched with
the feathers of the Valkan zim korf can do."

"As Erthyr is my witness."

Trumpets pealed. Everyone ran off to their posts.
Korero closed up at my back and nothing was going
to shift him from there. Volodu the Lungs spat and
wiped the mouthpiece of his battered lump of a
trumpet. Cleitar the Standard shook out my battle
flag, the flag fighting men call Old Superb. Ortyg the
Tresh lifted the Union Flag of Vallia. Well, we were
ready as we would be . . .

Flutduins lifted away. Their riders glittered in the
shafts of light from Zim and Genodras. Vollers swept

up into the air. We might be outnumbered two to one; we had air support and that would tip the balance.

If it did not—an exit and a quietus for us all.

What came to be known as the Battle of Marndor thus began in a most messy and ill-disciplined fashion.

Jhansi, too, had an air component. He had hired mercenaries riding fluttrells, those awkward birds with the ridiculous headvane that can so unsettle a flyer upon their backs. These swept up in a cloud to meet our own flyers.

Our soldiers tumbled out of our ships, formed their ranks, slanted their weapons. The vollers swept aloft and turned, keeping formation, lining out to rain fire and destruction down upon the heads of the enemy.

Our aerial cavalry might be airborne and surging forward into action; our ground cavalry was in an altogether different state. We had employed properly equipped vessels to transport the saddle animals, ships with stalls and pens and as much comfort as we could contrive. The gale had thoroughly upset the animals. They were refractory, unwilling to leave their pens, kicking and squealing. Only a few burs' time in which to quiet down would have made the difference. As it was, we were going to have to fight this battle with precious little ground cavalry.

I was almost in a mind to order the cage-ships aloft again and get them out of the way. But Jiktar Mophrey, commanding the totrix heavies, pleaded for a chance, and so I relented and he went back to his ships cursing and yelling and waving his riding crop in a veritable fury of determination to get into action.

Here, again, even in this fraught moment, I could review the anomalous situation that here in our army, which was so short of animals, my guards possessed two animals each man—and yet that seemed necessary. The guards performed work astride their zorcas which they could not riding nikvoves.

The commanders of the guards had sized up the situation and seen that this day they'd have to fight as infantry. This they could do supremely well. I stood to watch them form and march out, rank on rank, gleaming, magnificent, marching as one.

"That's where I should be," I said, fretfully, to Korero.

"Maybe. And maybe a commander should be where he can direct the battle."

Sharp, Korero, the golden Kildoi. His two massive shields slanted over me, borne indifferently in any of his four hands or his hand tail. If a shaft winged in past that defense, it was more likely to hit Korero than me, and chafe though I might, this was decreed—by Korero the Shield.

"When I blow," said Volodu, "they'll hear me better here."

Grumpily, I agreed. But I made a compact with myself that when the time came, I'd be up there with the lads, charging home. When I did, my small retinue would be in there with me, hollering and whooping with the best.

The first headlong onslaught of Jhansi's cavalry was checked, as it should have been checked, by our own dustrectium.* Then I saw his Bowmen of Loh moving up. They marched soldily, compact, rank on rank. I estimated he had close to five hundred archers there, a full regiment.

Seg had to reduce them to give us the chance

---

*Dustrectium. Firepower as applied to archery and engines.

to strike back. His Valkan Archers, elated at their success over the charging cavalry, licked their lips and settled down to serious shooting.

The contest was not to be decided by archery alone. From the air our vollers swooped down. Archers shot. Varters twanged and rocks hurtled down. Fire pots spat and sizzled.

Well, as you know I have fought on battlefields that were lost. I have been routed from the field. But, to the honor of Vallia, we had been in the habit of winning our battles recently. This one was going to be closely run.

The massed blocks of Bowmen of Loh did not relish the aerial attack. Many of them shot upwards. Superb archers though they truly are, even Bowmen of Loh have difficulty giving a true account of their prowess against swiftly darting targets swirling bewilderingly above them. When Seg's Valkan Archers loosed into the blocks, we could all see the gruesome results.

The massed ranks of Bowmen swayed. In only moments they were broken. In a rush, they routed off.

We all cheered, unrecking of the horror going on as men fled in blind panic from that field of blood.

Dismayed though Jhansi must have been at the sight of the flower of his infantry thus summarily dismissed, he did not waver. A second great cavalry charge roared in.

This was treated as harshly as the first.

His aerial cavalry had all been seen off, the fluttrells stumbling against the sky to escape. Now our flutduins came winging back, sharp bright points to inflict more grievous wounds on the forces below.

"He still has his infantry," said Korero.

"Aye. He must pay well. They stand firmly enough."

"Not masichieri, I'll warrant."

"No. Volodu, do you blow 'Phalanx Advance'?"

All Volodu did in answer was to put his battered trumpet to his lips and fairly blow a call that pierced shrillingly through all the hubbub.

Instantly the trumpets of the Kerchuri took up the call. Each of the six Jodhris forming the Kerchuri blew the advance, and each of the six Relianches forming a Jodhri echoed that thrilling impulse forward. The phalanx moved. It was not a full Phalanx, a Kerchuri only, yet it shook the ground. The helmets all came down, the shields slanted at the regulation angle. The pikes snouted forward in a bristle of death. The phalanx moved.

On the flanks the Hakkodin with their halberds and two-handed swords guarded any attempt to penetrate the formation. The chodku of archers covered the brumbytes with a sleeting umbrella of shafts.

Alongside the phalanx the heavy infantry, the churgurs, sword and shield men, advanced in their ponderous and yet deceptively swift gait. The whole force advanced.

It was not over yet.

Jhansi had more men than did we. He fought them well, but he could not handle the air.

When the phalanx hit his infantry it was as though a maddened bull burst through a flimsy garden fence.

Splinters of his infantry spun away. The plain was covered with running men throwing away sword and shield, spear and bow. The phalanx stormed after them.

Over the solid files waved the battle flags, and the pike heads gleamed and glittered in the radiance of the suns.

We had lost our spearmen in the gale. We followed up the wreck of Jhansi's army for a space, and then the recall blew. We had no light infantry, kreutzin to chase and harry the rout, no cavalry to make sure no further stand was made.

We scarcely needed them.

From the air, from voller and flutduin, the ruin below was harassed, pursued, given no rest.

We could let them get on with that until the Suns of Scorpio sank beneath the horizon.

Now we could get our breath back and take stock. Now would come the grim reckoning.

Deflated, drained, I turned away from that dying scene.

Thus ended the Battle of Marndor.

CHAPTER FIFTEEN

IN THE FLETCHER'S TOWER OF THE FALNAGUR

Turko the Khamorro picked me up, twirled me around, and slammed me down on the mat.

He stood back, hands on hips, and laughed hugely.

"You're getting soft, Dray Prescot! Your muscles are turning to water! Your resolution leaks away like the snows in spring!"

I pushed up, breathing hard, and glared.

"You are right, Turko, damned right. I am grown soft in these latter days. But, my friend—"

And I started after him.

A supreme example of perfection in musculature, Turko. He had a damned handsome face, too, bright and merry, knowing with a way that mocked and cut me down to size. The Khamorros, from the land of Herrell way down south in Havilfar, are famed and feared. It is whispered that they know secrets by which they may break and crush a man's bones. They so do.

No Khamorro is frightened to go up against a man wielding a weapon. In matters of the martial arts they reign supreme, alongside the Martial Monks of Djanduin and one or two other coteries of people who understand the Disciplines and the way of the hand's edge. They are supreme in all of Havilfar, with the Martial Monks. I remain convinced from my own personal knowledge that the Disciplines of the Krozairs of Zy give the Krozairs the edge. But very very few folk of Havilfar or of the other eastward lands of the grouping called Paz visit or know of the existence of the inner sea of Turismond, the Eye of the World.

So in the salle of the palace Turko and I tried a few falls. And it was as it usually was—in the end Turko was flat and, glaring up with that mocking laughter in his face, cried out: "Very well, Dray. I bare the throat. Perhaps you are not so decrepit, after all."

There was no answer to that. So I said, "Let us go up to your Fletcher's Tower and have a wet. Seg will be waiting."

We toweled down after standing for long enough under the showers. With robes slung casually about us we left the salle and crossed to the Fletcher's Tower. This had once been called the Jade Tower before Seg, when he was kov here, renamed it. We were in what Turko called his palace. This was, in truth, the castle-fortress of the Falnagur, which dominated the capital city of Falanriel.

"I own I'm surprised you didn't give the Fletcher's Tower a new name, Turko."

"Names outside Herrelldrin mean little, Dray. And, you will no doubt take the first opportunity to mock me, I sometimes wear a sword—"

I was truly astounded.

"You do what?"

"Oh, aye, I do."

I shook my head.

"Ice should freeze in a Herrelldrin Hell."

"Things have changed for me since you made me the Kov of Falinur."

"For the better, I am convinced, once we've got Jhansi off our necks."

"I wish I'd been with you at that little dust-up. Are you really going to call it the Battle of Marndor?"

"For myself, I wouldn't bother. But it was a fight. Men were killed. There was bravery. The men deserve it."

"Medals, you mean?"

"Why not? It was worth a bob to be worn with pride upon the chest."

"Agreed."

Turko had, as we suspected, been driven in with his army wing, and had sent to change the meeting place. The results of that were lying in hospital. The trouble was that now that Jhansi, with his confounded pact with the Racters to his north, could hire mercenaries from overseas, he could bring much greater forces to bear. The frontier between Vennar to the west and Falinur to the east ran north and south in a virtually indefensible line. Jhansi could pick his place to hit, hit and run. Turko had been doing very well in clearing out Falinur. Now all that work looked as though it had gone for nothing.

The battlemented fortress of the Falnagur had been taken in a furious onslaught, a coup de main, and now Turko could lord it in his own provincial capital. As we went through into the inner ward and up through narrow winding stairs, I recalled visiting Seg here. Times change, times change. Then Seg's wife Thelda could do nothing but prate about Queen Lushfymi of Lome. Now Thelda was happily married to Lol Polisto, the old emperor was dead, and Queen Lush was actively trying to marry my son Drak.

As to where Thelda might be now—well, tsleetha-tsleethi, as they say, softly-softly. That information might unsettle Seg. But, no! Of course not. Seg had thought Thelda dead and gone to the Ice Floes of Sicce. That she was alive and happy with Lol Polisto had brought him a kind of peace, for in Milsi Seg had found the perfect partner.

Kapt Erndor joined us as we went into the private snug.

"Hai, Erndor!" I said, shaking hands. "I am right glad to see you."

"Lahal, strom. We are in a pickle here, as you can see. But, now that you are here—"

"Kov Seg and I bring few regiments."

"I was not, strom, referring to regiments."

I'd guessed he wasn't. But these old Freedom Fighters of Valka, who take such pride in calling me strom instead of majister, they take a lot of beating. They are so hard, so gritty. Kapt Erndor, now, who had fought shoulder to shoulder with me when we cleared out Valka, he could roll between two millstones and grind them to powder.

For all that, Valkans are a lighthearted lot of rascals, ever ready to sing a song and drown a sorrow, to take their jug and wave it in the air as they yodel, as to brandish their swords . . .

Seg called out: "I've poured. It's a real Jholaix."

"By Morro the Muscle!" exclaimed Turko. "What it is to be married to a lady of a wine family of Jholaix."

Seg looked up as we went in. He was just finishing pouring the wine. Milsi and he had brought cases of the superb vintage after their second marriage in Jholaix. That had all gone off well, and Milsi's family had welcomed Seg. That there might be other rea-

sons for that could be gone into later. Right now,
Seg's and Milsi's bounty waited to be tasted.

"Superb!" pronounced Erndor, and his grim face
cracked into a broad smile.

"And the news is bad," said Seg. He'd just returned from a private reconnaissance of the lands of
which he had once been kov. What he told us made
us frown.

"You are only confirming what I already know,
Seg." Turko sipped carefully. "But I am glad you can
verify what I say. I know I must sound depressing."

"Not depressing, Turko," I said, sharply. "Realistic.
You've done extraordinarily well up here in Falinur.
But for that damned pact—"

"Well, can't we sabotage that?"

Seg was looking around this room. Once he had
lived here with Thelda. I said nothing, could say
nothing; I just trusted he was himself.

Turko's ideas of decoration had changed the room.
There was a single bow upon the wall, a single sword,
a single spear. Pelts covered much of the masonry.
Of pictures, Turko possessed a collection of action
poses of people throwing each other about. Of statues he had a few silver ones, most of bronze, and
these, too, were of men and women wrestling.

The tables were well provided with food and wines.
The chairs were deep and comfortable. We could
talk and argue and plan here all night.

A flick-flick plant upon the windowsill curled its
tendrils, seeking flies to pop down its orange cone.
Turko had imported some pleasant-smelling blooms
which stood about in pots of Pandahem ware. I sat
down, stretched out my naked feet, and took up
Seg's Jholaix.

"Here's to Milsi," I said.

We all solemnly drank. By Krun! It was good!

"Now let's find a way of bashing Jhansi."

Erndor rolled out the map upon a cleared space on the table. We all sat looking at it, and, I own, not a little glumly.

"I," I said, "have not a single idea in my stupid vosk-skull of a head."

"One thing," said Seg. "The Ninth Army is in good heart despite the setbacks."

"Oh, aye," confirmed Erndor. "They keep up, they keep up. But I wonder how much longer they can go on being pushed back from territory so hardly won."

"What information do you get from your spies, Turko?" I eyed him alertly. "If we could receive timely news just where that cramph Jhansi intends to attack—"

"Many men and women have been sent. We get scrappy information back. The last two pieces of news were false."

"He's penetrated your apparat there, and misleads you."

"Yes. We marched out to where we expected to find his army, and he crept in behind our backs and sacked two towns."

"A bad business."

A silver bowl of squishes stood on the table. I picked out one of the little fruits, looked at it, then deposited it where it filled my mouth with taste.

"Aye," said Turko. "I'd like to see Inch again. We communicate and he fights like a demon for his Black Hills."

"With Inch and you, Turko," said Seg, fretfully, "we ought to crush Jhansi like a rotten nut."

"It seems to me," I said, "that the days when we

were all wandering adventurers, seeking our fortunes
in the wide world, are all over. Now you're kovs, with
lands and responsibilities—" I stopped. Then I said,
"At least, Inch is a Kov with a fight on his hands,
you, Turko, are here with your back against the
wall—"

"And I am without lands," said Seg. "Well, that
does not worry me."

Quite casually, I said, "You are marked to be the
Hyr Kov of Balkan when the present incumbent dies
off, for he has no heirs."

Turko and Erndor had the sense to remain silent.

Seg fetched up a breath. "I am supposed to be the
King of Croxdrin. That means only that if it makes
Milsi happy, so be it. We shall go back there from
time to time. But Balkan? They always keep out of
trouble."

"Precisely. They serve only themselves up there.
It's a rich province. You'll do nicely up there, Seg,
and if, like me, you're a permanent absentee landlord,
then they'll keep the place going and the cash rolling
into your coffers."

"It is generous—hell, no, that's not what I mean."

"Well, drink up this splendid Jholaix your wife has
kindly provided, and let us get back to thinking of
ways of bashing Jhansi."

"I'll speak to you later about this, my old dom, by
the Veiled Froyvil, yes!"

So we talked more about Turko's problems. I should
mention here that Balkan is pronounced with both
a's flat, rhyming with ashcan. It was no ashcan of a
province, though; Balkan was an immensely rich Hyr
Kovnate. Its schturval was brown and red, its symbol
an eagle.

As I sipped the splendid wine and the talk drifted

on I found myself reflecting on just how funny a lot it was to be an emperor. The powers of such a one may appear enormous to the uninitiated. The truth is, as I have pointed out, the powers vary with strength and character, with the influence of other governing bodies, with factions, with the goodwill of the populace, with business and banking interests. Many an emperor takes the estates of deceased nobles who have no heirs into his own hands. He may then, if he pleases, bestow them upon loyal friends. How easy, it may seem, just to say to dear old Seg: "You are the Hyr Kov of Balkan!"

Well, in the ferocious and pragmatic ways of Kregen, Seg might have to fight for his new kovnate.

The talk turned then and drew me back.

"With the new accretion of flyers," Kapt Erndor was saying just as the knock came on the door, "I can set up a reasonably efficient system of aerial patrols."

The door opened to admit Nath na Kochwold, looking dusty. He made a gesture with his fingers, pointing to his mouth. Laughing, Seg hoisted a jug and Nath took it, swallowed, wiped his mouth, said: "By Vox! It's like a night of Notor Zan out there!"

"All to rights?"

"Aye. The lads are all tucked in. And, I can tell you, there were only four fights among the different Kerchuris. Remarkable." He drank again and glanced at Erndor. "These aerial patrols. To cover the entire border they'll have to be spread very thinly."

"Very."

"Still," said Seg cheerfully. "There must be well-known routes. I recall reconnoitering over there and thinking it was open land. But there must be well-trodden ways we can omit."

"True."

"If you'll release the flutduins to me, strom, I'll set up a system first thing."

"Excellent, Erndor, excellent."

Nath said: "It is a great pity the fleet has had to return to Vondium. We do not really have enough aerial transports to get a large enough force into action quickly enough."

"That" pointed out Turko, "caused my retreat and you your Battle of Marndor."

"H'm," I said. "Maybe we can persude Farris to spare us a voller or two. I am sorry that Deb-Lu-Quienyin had to return to Vondium. He is a comfort."

They did not reply; but drank. They all knew exactly what I meant.

"If you'll pardon me, strom, I'll turn in. I have a heavy day tomorrow."

"And us all, I think."

Erndor left, saying his good nights, and Seg, standing tall and powerful in the room, downed the last of his wine. Nath na Kochwold poured the last of the bottle.

"I'll just finish this. There are details I wish to talk over with Turko."

So Seg and I left together. We'd been quartered in a fine accommodation block across the courtyard. The stone entrance was guarded by one of Turko's men and also by a kampeon from 1ESW. They saluted as we bid them good night. The entrance hall was carpeted, and featured jars of Pandahem ware, an over-life-size statue of a dancing talu, heavy sturm-wood chairs and a wide table where visitors might deposit their cloaks. The carpet felt thick underfoot.

Seg yawned.

"I shan't be sorry to get to sleep, my old dom. See you in the morning." With that he ran fleetly up the stairs. He almost collided with a girl coming down. She wore a yellow apron and carried a brass tray whereon reposed a half-flagon and two jugs, besides a dish of palines.

With his habitual gallantry, Seg apologized, made sure the girl was all right, and then went leaping on up.

She passed me with eyes she intended to be downcast, but she could not resist a single liquid glance up. I managed a grimace that might pass for a smile, and said, "The guards are grateful that you look after them, believe me."

She colored up, managed a mouselike: "Yes, majister," and skipped outside. Her slippers were red with pretty white bows.

I'd reached the top of the stairs when I heard the crash from outside. Stopping, one hand on the balustrade, I turned to look down into the entrance hall.

The lamps threw scattered illumination across the carpet, picked out the fantastic decoration on one rotund jar. The blooms filled the air with a perfume at once heady and sharp.

Through the open door two sounds reached me, mingled together in horrid counterpoint.

One—the terrified screaming of a girl. The other— the snarling growl of a beast.

I started down the stairs like a madman.

Halfway down, I saw the gray feral form leaping after the girl who struggled to run and who fell asprawl across that luxurious carpet.

In the next second the werewolf would sink those long yellow fangs into that soft body.

There was only one thing I could do.

With a ferocious yell I plunged down the stairs, ripping out my sword, that useless sword of steel.

CHAPTER SIXTEEN

A CORPSE SPEAKS

Steel! *Steel!* Useless . . .

That beautiful drexer fashioned in the armories of Valka, designed to take all the best of the Havilfarese thraxter, the Vallian clanxer and what we could contrive of the Savanti Sword—all that skill and cunning, that knowledge and craft—all wasted, impotent, useless . . .

I went down the stairs so fast I almost pitched onto my nose. The werewolf saw me. His eyes, reddened in the lamps' glare, seemed to shoot sparks. The saliva that dripped between his fangs hung thick and clotted. He panted. He looked what he was, vicious and deadly and utterly without understanding of human mercy.

He leaped the girl to get at me. He snarled up the stairs, lips drawn back blackly to bare those curved sharp fangs. His hair spiked in a thick bristle about his neck. Oh, yes, as I went hurtling down I could see he was a very devil of a werewolf.

The penultimate step before I'd be on him—or he on me—I took off. I jumped. I soared clean over his back and landed cat-footed on the carpet beyond. With a growl from some blasphemous bowel-region he swiveled about. In the heartbeat before he turned

I slashed the sword at him, sliced deeply into his hind leg.

He screeched—who wouldn't?—and swung away. My second blow sizzled past his nose as he went back.

The wound in his hind leg affected his agility in no way at all. He seemed not to have been touched.

With a guttural explosion of sound he leaped again.

This time I contrived to roll under and to the side and as I went I gave him the old leem-hunter's trick.

Had he been a leem, even, one of the fiercest of all Kregen's predators, his guts would have spilled out through that long slicing slash along his belly. I saw blood ooze. I saw it, I swear. But he landed on the carpet, screeching, and cocked that lean body around to get at me once more.

In this oddly one-sided combat, weird and uncanny, there was no raw stink of spilled blood. I've fought many a wild beast, as you know, and have developed techniques for dealing with the different species—to my shame, I add, for a number of them merely fight so savagely because that is their nature—and by this time any four-legged animal of this wolfish mold, large though he be, would have been done for.

When the ganchark charged again I caught the distinct impression that he was as speedy as an ordinary wolf, a fast one, admittedly. I did not think I'd slowed him at all by my blows.

This time I tried a new ploy and smashed him full across the muzzle. He yelped and catapulted past to the right as I slid to the left. Again no wound appeared.

Only a moment or two had elapsed since I'd rushed so recklessly down the stairs. The girl lay in a swoon, and we antagonists circled her to get at each other.

He came on, I struck and slid, and once more he charged. This could go on all night . . .

In a few moments more Seg would come roaring down and that prospect alarmed me and nerved me to make an end quickly—but how?

He came at me headlong, muzzle agape, and I struck more to fend him off than to try to hurt him. Where the guards at the door were was probably down wandering among the Ice Floes of Sicce.

The next attack saw me crash sideways into a gorgeous jar of Pandahem ware. It went over with a smash. Bits of ceramic sprayed. I dodged sideways and nearly did myself a serious injury on the outspread fingers of the dancing talu.

My left hand gripped the bicep of one of the statue's eight arms. I held myself straight to face the next attack—and then I realized.

Fool! Onker! Get onker! Of course!

Now it had to be arranged. The stoppered vial in my pouch remained intact. I reached in, fumbled about, and drew it forth. If I dropped it now, when the ganchark, slavering, leaped again . . .

I dodged away, swiveling, fending the thing off and yet not allowing myself to remain in the path of his leap. His teeth looked mightily unpleasant. Again I circled to the statue of the dancing talu. The eight arms, extended in that familiar wagon wheel of abandonment, were fashioned, like the trunk and legs, of bronze. The head, all artful secret smiles, was of gold.

But the fingernails . . .

I smeared the ganjid on as many fingernails as I could reach on that pass, slashed nastily at the werewolf and saw a chunk of gray fur fly. That was about as much as I could hurt him—yet. More ganjid smeared over other fingernails. I drew out, dropped the vial, poised.

Seg's yell reached me from the stairs.

"Dray!"

"Stand back, Seg!"

The werewolf leaped. I waited, flashed the sword as I had flashed it so many times before in his reddened eyes, and then skipped sideways. But, this time, I drove the sword full at his face and let go. It slid into an eye. I felt it go in as I went sideways.

He paused, shrieking, and then . . .!

The sword began to ease out of his eye. Bodily, it moved back. He stood trembling, his tongue hanging, as the sword was pushed out of his eye by supernatural forces and dropped with a thud upon the carpet.

He snarled now as though admitting that the thrust would have killed a lesser beast, a savage animal who was not were . . .

He leaped.

I took the over-life-size statue of the dancing talu by two of his lower arms and I lifted him and turned him. I held him angled forward. The ganchark leaped at me and hurtled straight onto a hedge fashioned from the dudinter fingers of the statue.

Later we counted the number of fingernails that pierced him.

Five.

Five electrum fingernails coated with wolfsbane, five of them, they did for him, all right.

Seg raced down into the hall, yelling. Other people appeared and if they'd been watching then I did not fault them. They'd had the courage in that case not to run away. We stood in a ring looking at the werewolf, and two of the girls bent over the limp form of the serving girl.

"The puncture lady's coming," said a Pachak wearing his badge of office.

We watched.

Who would lie revealed when the evil occult force leached away from that fearsome gray form?

The gray fur shimmered, the fierce head rounded, the form softened until the body of the guard who had stood at the entrance and bid us good night lay on the carpet.

"Larghos m'Mondifer," I said. He was a doughty kampeon who had recently been enrolled as a jurukker in 1ESW.

Then something happened for which we were totally unprepared.

The corpse opened its eyes.

Before anyone could scream or faint, the mouth opened. A sighing of air, as of the opening of a long-disused tomb, and then the corpse of Larghos m'Mondifer spoke.

"This, Dray Prescot, was not my doing."

Now the screams rang out, now the fainting ones slid to the carpet.

The body of Larghos m'Mondifer turned black. The skin shone like enamel, then dulled to ash. Cracks appeared running all over in a spiderweb. The guardsman collapsed. He fell in on himself, and then only an outline in black dust showed on that thick carpet, and then that whisked away and there was nothing left of a fine fighting man of Vallia who had been changed into a werewolf.

CHAPTER SEVENTEEN

THE EMPEROR OF VALLIA'S WEREWOLVES

The Werewolf of Vondium, then, had not been alone . . .

Stringent inquiries revealed nothing to distinguish poor Larghos m'Mondifer from any other of the guard corps. He'd done his duty, stood his guard, fought well in the Battle of Marndor. I just didn't like the way the two werewolves had been members of my own bodyguard.

And just what was a corpse doing, spouting mysteries?

Seg said, "We were told, Milsi and me, that there were werewolves up along the plains of Northern Croxdrin. Werewerstings, they were supposed to be."

Marion cocked her head at him at this. Nath na Kochwold looked grim. We were taking our usual second breakfast standing up and nobody was feeling at all cheerful.

"What the hell did that poor fellow mean?" demanded Turko.

"He spoke my name. A dead man. All right, I am at a loss. If Deb-Lu is engaged on his own weighty affairs we must send for Khe-Hi-Bjanching right away."

Khe-Hi was down in the southwest with Drak. I'd not argue about calling him, for this mystery deepened and we needed a Wizard of Loh.

In the days that followed we went about our business in a dour, almost sullen way. There were two more werewolf attacks that left the victims with torn-out throats.

We sent for the dudinter weapons from Vondium.

Khe-Hi-Bjanching, red-haired, his austerely handsome face a trifle plumper in these latter days, arrived by fast voller. He was abreast of the situation. Wizards of Loh have their means of communication.

In his chiseled-steel voice he said, "I have the ganjid recipe and will begin at once, majister. This is a bad business. Rumors fly wildly all over Vallia."

"Rumors won't sink supernatural fangs into you, Khe-Hi."

"There are facets to this business that intrigue me. Deb-Lu has a great deal on at the moment."

I wasn't going to pry into what was going on between these two puissant wizards. They were friends. I was convinced about that, and they had both served Vallia and me well in the past. Khe-Hi went off to the kitchens and his acolytes began the collection of the necessaries.

There would be no fumbling in the gathering of ingredients required by Khe-Hi. Oh, no! A deal younger than Deb-Lu, his powers grew every season, or so it seemed. I had known him longer than Deb-Lu, and because Delia had told me to pull him out of a hole, he fancied he owed me a debt. We had talked around this, and I think both had come to the understanding that our friendship and mutual loyalty reached a much higher level than mere gratitude.

Looking back at those infuriating days spent in Falinur trying to hold the border, to repel Layco Jhansi and to deal with the damned werewolves, I recall an oppressive feeling of bafflement. I was frustrated at every turn. We put out aerial patrols and we caught a number of raids. Everyone did their work well. The soldiers flew or marched and got stuck in. We held Jhansi, and even put in a few raids on our own account.

But—everywhere the Emperor of Vallia went, there went also the werewolves.

This became patently obvious

We caught three more of the poor fellows. All three were from my own guard corps.

I began seriously to consider sending 1ESW and 1EYJ back to Vondium or to Drak.

Then a particularly nasty outbreak occurred when we were up north chasing a retreating raid. We'd surprised the devils as they burned a farm. Afterwards, when we rested around the ruins of the farm, no fewer than four of the local girls were killed in that nauseatingly familiar way. Their throats were uniformly ripped out.

We laid a trap. We caught the unholy ganchark.

And he turned out to be Nalgre the Rear, a member of Turko's select body of personal guards.

Andrinos, the Khibil wrestler who was now on very good terms with Turko, shook his head, pursing up his lips as we stood looking down on the body.

"This bodes no good—" he began.

"Wait, Andrinos. Let us see if he speaks."

But no other corpse than that of Larghos m'Mondifer opened his eyes and mouth and spoke to me—so far . . .

In those evil days much of the old Dray Prescot returned. I saw more than one man flinch away when I looked quite reasonably at him. The atmosphere grew strained. We were overstretched, true; but that was no new thing, that was almost always the norm.

By chance one rainy evening I overheard a conversation through a tent flap. Eavesdroppers never hear good, as they say.

Two soldiers out of one of Turko's regiments were talking in that low-voiced rumble that indicates they are old friends, and have no fear of being overheard.

"I tell you, Nath, the land is accursed."

"That's true, by Vox. And all since this Kov Seg returned. He was thrown out before—"

"Aye. But Kov Turko is harsher against the slave-masters."

"That may be, Mondo. But it is certain sure this Seg was infected by werewolves in his own kingdom, wherever in some foreign devil-land that may be. He said so himself."

I rounded the corner of the tent-flap, stepped over the guy-rope, and said, "Stand up. Attention."

They saw who I was. They scrambled up. They tried to stand to attention, and made a poor hash of it for the trembling fits that seized them.

"I shall not have you flogged, or beaten, or tortured, nor even have you neatly put to death. I will tell you this. Kov Seg Segutorio is not the cause of this plague of werewolves. He is not a sorcerer. Had he been, perhaps you would have been turned into little green toads for your stupidity."

They stood there. They looked ghastly. No thought of trying to make a run for it entered their heads, and certainly no thought of trying to tackle me would even reach them—they knew what the Krozair longsword across my back could do.

That I would have used that superb brand was certain sure. These were the rumors that were doing so much to destroy the credibility of myself and my friends

The two, Nath and Mondo, I dismissed with a few final words of caution. Then I added an admonition to cheer up, for we were bound in the end to triumph over the gancharks. They trailed off looking as though they'd fallen off a cliff onto the rocks beneath.

I hadn't touched them physically, but that old face that transforms me, the face men call the devil face of Dray Prescot, must have flamed out in all its evil power.

The decision not to tell Seg what I had overheard could easily be made; implementing it was quite different.

As we flew back to Falanriel, Seg remarked in his deceptively casual way: "These rumors are flying thicker than flies around a corpse."

"So it seems."

The breeze blew in our faces, the suns shone, the air smelled sweet with that particular sweetness only found on Kregen, yet I felt the chill of unease.

"Yes, my old dom. Seems people are blaming you directly. I've had a few words with 'em."

That I could imagine.

So I told Seg what Nath and Mondo had said.

"Oh, yes, sure. I've heard that, too. But they lay the blame on your shoulders, Dray, because everywhere you go the werewolves appear."

"Just a coincidence."

Seg squinted off at the horizon.

"Maybe, Dray, and maybe not."

I remained silent. Seg, I knew, had had a thought.

He went on: "We may not know if this is true or not, but let us assume for a moment that it is. We may never know just why it is. But, if it should be so then surely it will give us a lead, a chance, a lever to use against the dratted werewolves. Yes?"

"If it be so, if this unholy thing you're suggesting is true, then how do we use it?"

"I'll have a few words on that score with Khe-Hi."

I faced him. "Yes, Seg. Yes. Do that. I own the whole evil business is getting me down."

A sad incident occurred shortly after we touched down.

One of the girls who had been so gruesomely slain by a werewolf—and, of course, we could not tell if the werewolves we caught were the ones who had committed the crimes—had been just such a young, carefree lass as to warm the heart of the crustiest old curmudgeon. Pansi the Song, that was her name. She'd worked in a tavern of good repute in Falanriel, and she'd been found torn to pieces in a back alley.

Her father, Nolro the Abrupt, a thickly built man with a luxuriant mop of brown Vallian hair and an abdomen rotund yet solid, took his daughter's death ill. He must have heard the stories and rumors circulating so wildly. He must have brooded. His wife was long since dead. After Sasfri had been taken from him, all his hopes and affections centered on Pansi the Song.

And now she was dead, dreadfully killed by a werewolf brought to Falanriel by the emperor.

We walked from the voller and Nolro the Abrupt, crazed by grief, desperate, hurled himself through the ranks and bore down on me brandishing a thick iron bar.

Thank Zair there was nothing physical and immediate I had to do, save shout: "Do not harm him!"

My lads closed up and took the iron bar away.

Nolro was screaming hysterically, all his bulk shaking.

"Werewolf lover! Murderer! Death to the emperor!"

I said to Jiktar Vandur: "See to him, Vandur. Fetch a needleman. Try to treat him gently. When he is calm I shall visit him."

"Quidang!" Vandur, as tough as they come, with a chestful of bobs, pulled his moustache. "Although I give you odds, majister, against his full recovery."

"I hope you are wrong. But I fear you may be right."

"If I catch these rumor mongers I'll string 'em up and have their tripes out, by the Blade of Kurin!"

So, as you may easily imagine, I was not a happy man as we went up into the Fletcher's Tower. It seemed to me that the werewolves and the rumors were alienating me from the populace. The very people who had cried for me as Jak the Drang and then as Dray Prescot to become their emperor and get them out of their troubles were now baying for my blood.

Later on Jiktar Vandur sent word that Nolro the Abrupt was quieted down. The doctors had stuck him all over with acupuncture needles, and he could hear and speak coherently. I went down to the little medical room where he lay in bed. His wrists and ankles were tied to the bed. At this I felt a leaden thump of my spirits.

"Majister," he said, "as you can see, I cannot give you the full incline."

As sarcasm it was lost on me. But it gave me an opening. I said in what I hoped was a cool yet friendly voice: "You should know, Nolro, that I do not care for the full incline, and detest all this bowing and scraping. It seems you are deceived in your understanding of me."

"I do not misunderstand that my Pansi is dead or that where you go the werewolves go—"

I did not so much argue with him as cajole as though he were a fever patient. I pointed out the obvious; that as the confounded emperor I was hardly likely to cause this kind of suffering to the people when it harmed us all. His face clouded at this, and I could see he was chewing this simple-minded piece of logic over in his mind

Then: "But the werewolves appear wherever you go . . ."

"That I do not deny, Nolro. I deny I cause them."

He shook his head fretfully. "But it is one and the same."

I said, "You have the grief of a lost daughter upon your shoulders. I know how you feel." And, by Zair, I did . . .

He pulled at his bound wrists, but I went on quickly, thrusting those old ugly thoughts away: "I have the grief of all the daughters, all the sons, upon my shoulders, Nolro."

We talked for a little more. The doctors were there, hovering in the background, and the guard, and an old cleaning lady stood by the door, her hands folded into her yellow apron. I thought Nolro was still in a state of shock at the death of Pansi the Song; but that he now understood that the reasons were not as simple as he imagined.

"I promise you, Nolro, as Opaz is my witness, we shall discover the evil secret of the gancharks. We shall make sure they cannot harm anyone else. I pledge you this, Nolro, and all the people of Falanriel, all the people of Vallia."

"I believe you, majister—"

I took out my knife, my old sailor knife I keep snugged over my right hip. I slashed his bonds. He looked startled and I was aware of a quick movement from the doctors, the guards, the old cleaning lady.

"Stand fast," I snapped without turning around.

I extended the knife hilt first to Nolro.

"If you condemn me, Nolro the Abrupt, then use this knife. Strike home and deliver justice!"

Well, by the Black Chunkrah! That was a dangerous gesture . . .

Nolro took the knife. I was interested to notice it did not quiver in his broad red hand. He looked at it. He looked up at me. With a great gulp of indrawn breath he hurled the knife down onto the bedclothes. His face was so twisted that I felt my own spirit twist in response.

There was no need for anything further. Retrieving the knife, I sheathed it. I went out without another word.

There was no need to tell anyone to spread this story. The witnesses would rush out to tell everyone they met what had passed between the Emperor of Vallia and Nolro the Abrupt.

And, for all that, nothing would bring back the smiles and the music of Pansi the Song . . .

CHAPTER EIGHTEEN

OF A VOLUNTEER FROM THE JIKAI VUVUSHIS

The ugly truth was that I must be to blame. Somehow wherever I went the damned werewolves appeared.

This could not be mere coincidence.

And the corpse of Larghos m'Mondifer speaking to me. I trembled to think just who might have been using his cadaver to communicate with me. If the idea I did not wish to allow into my head proved true, then, indeed, Vallia was in deep water.

During this period, as we attempted to prosecute the campaign against Layco Jhansi, I decided it would be best if I did not frequent Falanriel, or any town at all. Spending days in camp or on the march I hoped would deprive any potential werewolves from preying on simple young girls. In this I was proved right. But the attrocities continued, and soldiers were ripped to shreds on guard duty. We caught the werewolves. Useless to place two men or a girl and a man on duty. One so often became a werewolf and destroyed the other. We mounted guard by audo, by a section of eight or ten men, and still, as is the awkward nature of humankind, the werewolves appeared and caught men on their own. Despite the strictest orders there were still those foolish enough to go off alone.

One example showed us the way of it.

Three men detached were all good comrades, men who had fought together in the files and trusted one another with their lives. One went to fetch the wine, keeping in full view of the tent, under observation at all times. When this man, Fonrien the Latch, returned to the tent he found one of his comrades, Nath Furman, dead with dreadful wounds, and the werewolf just running wildly off. When the pursuit eventually gave up, the third comrade, Nugos the Unwary, trailed in covered in blood with some story of chasing after the ganchark.

The case seemed open and shut.

"Suppose," said Nath na Kochwold—for the men were brumbytes—"Suppose Nugos the Unwary is not the ganchark? How can we slay him in cold blood?"

"The proof seems very clear," said Decor. He stood imposingly in his pikeman's uniform, massive and bulging with muscle, his face hard as the edge of the kax covering his chest. Decor, as the Brumbytevax, shared Nath's concern for the phalanx. "It is cruel. But it must be done."

The marquee-like tent in which we gathered resounded in that dully flapping way of tents with the voices of the arguers. It seemed perfectly plain that the moment Fonrien the Latch, who was a brumbyte, had gone off to fetch the wine allowance, Nugos the Unwary, who was a Faxul, a leader of the file, had transmogrified himself into a werewolf. Then he had ripped out the throat of Nath Furman, who was the laik-faxul, and had sought to escape.

"This is a matter for the Phalanx," declared Brytevax Decor. "Acting under the orders of the emperor direct."

This was a typical hard-nosed attitude by a commander to keep his own affairs to himself. It implied the absence from the deliberations of Kov Turko and of Kapt Erndor. I fancied Turko would chafe at this, and then welcome the chance to distance himself from a nasty business. He was hard, was our Turko; but he was a man with a human heart, as I well knew.

The swiftly grown tradition of the Phalanx, inspired, guided, given impetus by me at a time when the fate of Vallia hung on the performance of untried troops using new-fangled weapons, had, indeed, blossomed into a marvelous growth. The Phalanx might not quite be a law unto itself, but it cherished its own ways, and fiercely defended its conduct, on the field and off. This is, I suppose, one of the prices one pays for creating an elite.

If one of the Phalanx was a damned unholy werewolf, then the Phalanx would deal with him. Queyd-arn-tung.

All the same—suppose Nugos the Unwary was not a werewolf?

Upon being asked simple leading questions, Nugos just shook his head. He replied openly enough; he remembered nothing from the moment Fonrien the Latch had gone to bring the wine to the moment he discovered himself, covered in blood, crawling along the ground. He supposed he must have chased after the werewolf, injured himself and lost all memory.

"That is a probability," said Nath na Kochwold.

They all knew, these tough men in the marquee, that the Emperor of Vallia did not countenance torture as a method of extracting information. The temptation to use that disgusting system did not tempt me even now.

I said, when Nugos had been carted off to the
guardtent: "We must try to use this to our own
advantage. Set up a hut—not a tent—with two
compartments. Let there be a spyhole. We will set
Nugos in one half and keep an observation on him
from the other. A strong guard at all times, of course."

"And who will be the bait?" Seg in his fey way
knew how to put his finger on the nub of the question.

"An audo of your lads with dudinter-tipped shafts
should stop him. The guard ready to rush in. Yes, I
think you might ask for volunteers from the Jikai
Vuvushis."

Well, distasteful though this was, it was done.

Poor Nugos the Unwary! Well-named, indeed!

A girl, lithe, splendidly formed, swinging along in
her battle-leathers, stepped forward. Minci Farndion,
a Deldar in the new guard regiment, unhesitatingly
volunteered. She was by a half a heartbeat only
quicker than her companions in the ranks

I expressed no wish to see the result of this nause-
ating experiment. The Phalanx, jealous of its position
and privileges, handled all. Minci stepped in alone,
carrying a tray with food. Poor Nugos transformed
himself and was instantly pierced by shafts and slashed
to ribbons by the dudinter blades of the guard who
rushed in from their hidden vantage points.

Well, as I say, if I was the cause of all this horror
and misery I'd reck little to the cost of clearing it all
up—but I could do without scenes like these, by
Krun.

Flinging ourselves into the task of dealing with
Layco Jhansi, we kept up the aerial patrols, and
caught two of his columns in ambushes. We felt a
distinct sense that he was growing cautious. We

planned for a bolder advance into the territory of Vennar.

At this time, too, news came that Natyzha Famphreon, the Dowager Kovneva of Falkerdrin, rallied against her illness. She still clung to life with the same stubbornness she had always shown. A tough and stringy old bird, Natyzha. Despite that she as an avowed Racter had stood against me, I owned to a feeling of loss in the world when she eventually passed on to wherever she was bound.

Khe-Hi reported that he, too, like Deb-Lu, was aware of these quick stabs of occult power from time to time.

"They come at random, San?"

"Yes, Dray. I think they must be connected with the ganchark phenomenon."

"So do I. But who—"

"If he was not dead, I'd have no hesitation in knowing just who, by Hlo-Hli."

"There is his wife and child."

"So it must be them."

"I fear so."

Khe-Hi pulled at the crimson cord cincturing his waist. His clean-shaven face looked both sad and grim. He said, "Deb-Lu and I have fashioned over the seasons a powerful defense for Vallia—and for yourself, as you know. But any defense, I suppose, may be pierced if the thrust is hard and concentrated enough."

"As for myself, I fancy the lady has taken to me. This is her misfortune. The child, the uhu Phunik, is the truly malignant power."

"You know of the love Csitra had for Phu-Si-Yantong? Yes. Ling-Li-Lwingling came along and turned his head. Deb-Lu has apprized you of these facts. If Csitra does truly imagine herself to be infatuated with you, Dray—and pardon me for putting it quite like that—she is a woman who will adhere rigidly to her own obsession."

"I suppose I ought to feel thankful."

"Oh, indeed, yes." The wizard's metallic voice held no levity. "If this is the handiwork of Phunik, Deb-Lu and I can handle him and his powers. It will take many seasons before he approaches anywhere near our combined kharrna."

"And Csitra?"

"We felt her assisting Yantong when we blew him away in the Quern of Gramarye. She has power. I think even with her uhu she cannot master us."

"Then," I said, and I spoke with more acerbity than I intended, "Then by the disgusting diseased left eyeball of Makki Grodno! Why do you not stop them?"

"I will reply to your perfectly reasonable question when I have consulted further with Deb-Lu."

The rebuke was merited.

I nodded perfunctorily, and Khe-Hi took himself off.

I, Dray Prescot, Lord of Strombor and Krozair of Zy, did not wish to turn into a veritable ogre. But, by Krun, these diabolical occult events were forcing me down that ugly path.

Mind you, as I went off to find Seg and Nath and have a wet and discuss plans for the forthcoming offensive, I reflected that there'd been something distinctly odd about Khe-Hi during this conversation. Now, just when was that? I found Seg and Nath in the mess tent, and I snatched up a glass at random, my mind working back on that conversation.

"Hai, Dray! You look as though you've lost a zorca and found a calsany."

"Something like that," I said, and then I had it.

The Wizard of Loh had looked decidedly shifty when he'd talked of Ling-Li-Lwingling, the Witch of Loh I'd met in Jikaida City in the center of Havilfar.

Now, why was that?

Nath resumed the conversation my entrance had interrupted. Strangely enough, this concerned Khe-Hi.

"We do not know the locus of infection, Khe-Hi was telling me. It might be anything. If a victim can be kissed by dudinter very soon afterwards, there is a chance he may be cured."

"It is safe?"

"Not at all. The transformation, I was told by those who witnessed it in Nugos, was exceedingly swift."

I said, "But he had been a werewolf before—for how long we do not know."

"The devil of it is," said Seg, "there could be a dozen of the dratted things prowling about out there right now."

That thought could unsettle anyone, could waft an icy draft of unease down any spine

We deliberately pushed those unwelcome thoughts aside and got down to serious planning. Seg, Turko, Nath, Kapt Erndor—any one of them alone could have planned out the forthcoming actions. I was not needed. As the emperor, it could be said, my place was at the center, at the fulcrum, in Vondium.

By Zair! I wasn't going anywhere near Vondium while my every footstep was dogged by these blasphemous werewolves, these ghastly visitations from malignant sorcerers. Not a chance, by Krun!

By chance I was aware of some work done on this Earth in connection with werewolves and the disease of lycanthropy. The myths and legends insisted that silver was the metal to dispose of the weremonsters. A test had been made of Nugos, a simple thing, when a dudinter ring had been slipped on his finger. He had not appeared disconcerted.

So we did not have that handy way of detecting the gancharks amongst us in human form. Mind you, any intelligent bloke who knows he's going to turn into a werewolf come full moon can always smear shellac or some similar coating onto his hands to pick up the silver candlestick.

We were all mightily heartened when Tom Tomor sent a regiment of Valkan Archers to join us, and two crack regiments of Pachaks from Zamra. Our strength grew slowly. As ever, we were short of saddle animals. Now if what I considered the unlikely schemes of my kregoinye comrade, Pompino the Iarvin, came to fruition, he ought to be sailing back to Vondium in his fine new galleon. He'd gone faring forth to Pandahem to bring hersanys, heavy, six-legged, chalk-white-haired beasts, from Seg and Milsi's kingdom of Croxdrin. I wondered if he'd run into any of the werewerstings up there Seg had mentioned.

Incidentally, I confess that although I had the comfort of Makki Grodno, I did miss the Divine Lady of Belschutz . . .

Well, all that rascally crew had sailed with Pompino. When he sailed back, if he ever did, and he had managed to procure saddle animals, no doubt shamelessly using the specialist merchant in saddle animals, Obolya Metromin, he would be mightily welcomed. Pompino, I fancied, would be pretty sharp with Obolya, calling himself the Zorcanim. Also, if I knew my Khibil comrade Pompino, he'd earn his nickname of the Iarvin by letting it be known that he was a personal friend of Jak Leemsjid, who just happened to be a personal friend of the King and Queen of Croxdrin.

These thoughts made me break in to ask Seg how his friends from Croxdrin fared in Vallia, to which he replied that the two pygmies, Diomb and Bamba, had been taken off by Milsi, and that the rest of his cutthroat bunch were either organizing themselves or being organized into the regiment I'd told him he ought to raise.

"They'll come in handy, Seg, when Balkan comes along. News is scant out of that hyr kovnate. I hope it all goes smoothly when the time comes."

Even as I spoke I knew that, this being Kregen, it would not go smoothly . . .

Letters came in and went out. I heard from Drak who said that Dayra had been through like a wind-storm. His sister, he said, was desirous of visiting his other sister, Lela, out in Havilfar. This astonished me.

Still no reasonable results were obtained with the werewolf business and we were, on that problem, as Seg said, like a pickpocket with no fingers.

We were pushing Layco Jhansi's forces back. In more than one conversation on the eve of battle it was suggested that after the coming victory we should push on to the town he had made his provincial capital, Vendalume.

"We catch the rast there, string him up, and the rest will fall into line," promised Turko. He had no need to swell his chest and bulge his muscles, as so many Khamorros did. He was grown in stature in quite unphysical ways, was Turko, in these latter days.

"Your spy network is working better now," I said.

We stood watching the twin suns set, Zim and
Genodras flooding down their mingled light upon the
stricken field where the medics worked devotedly.
The battle had been arduous, for we'd caught a sizable Jhansi force, and destroyed them. That was the
Battle of Farnrien's Edge. The new regiments had
fought magnificently, lost few casualties, and now
our lines resounded with victory celebrations. "I could
wish I had a certain barrel of a fellow to spy for us—"

"Naghan Raerdu?" Turko laughed. "Aye, I remem-
ber him, and the way he cried hot tears when he
laughed."

"An acute, brilliant and invaluable man, Turko."

"Well, we've done pretty well. And the news from
Inch is good."

"Yes. I rather thought—and I'll let you and Inch
sort it out—that we could split Vennar down the
middle. Half to you, half to Inch."

"That is not only fair, it is generous to both—"

"You'll both have to agree—"

"Of course. I see no problem at all, by Morro the
Muscle! With Inch on my western borders I'll sleep
well."

How quickly Turko had picked up the affectations
of nobility, of thinking like a kov!

The uproar from the lines continued. We'd left the
main camp a few miles to the rear with the tents and
impedimenta and the camp followers. We'd rest up
and then march back. The twin suns sank and the
Maiden with the Many Smiles, already aloft, poured
down her fuzzy pink radiance upon the land. As we
stood drinking in the cool night air shadows moved
out across the plain beyond the battlefield.

"What—?" said Turko.

Nath na Kochwold cantered across astride a zorca. He pointed out.

"The lurfings of the plain try to scavenge the dead—" He stopped himself and raised in the stirrups. He stared.

"Well?" snapped Turko.

"I think—by Vox! It is so! Many and many of them—"

I was jumping up onto a varter, climbing to balance on the ballista. I looked out across that moon-drenched landscape. Rosy light flooded down and the shadows lay long and undulating. And in that wash of fuzzy pink radiance there was no mistaking the nature of those hideous forms that leaped along in a baying pack.

Howling, a monstrous pack of them, their gray backs like a tidal rip, the werewolves poured past in a torrent, hell-bent on our undefended camp and all the camp-followers there.

CHAPTER NINETEEN

HOWLING UNDER
THE MOONS

There was nothing else to do but race like a madman for the zorca lines and fling myself across the first animal I laid hands on. She was a fine chestnut and she quieted instantly as I grasped her mane. Bareback, head low, feet tucked in, I roared off after that blasphemous rout.

Nath rode with me. Magically, Seg and Turko were there. Others joined us. Volodu was blowing his lungs out, shrilling the alarm over the entire camp.

In a straggling bunch, heads low, we raced after that streaming howling pack of werewolves.

Every man jack of us, I was sure, wore among the usual Kregan arsenal of weaponry a dudinter blade.

Nothing was going to outrun a zorca, on four, six or eight feet, or on two. Among the bunch of riders following me were men and women riding sleeths, two-legged dinosaurs, swarths, four-legged dinosaurs, totrixes, six-legged lumbering saddle animals of great stubbornness, zorcas with their four nimble feet and single upflung spiral horn, and there were even a few souls aboard nikvoves.

Roaring with the fury to get at the gancharks, we raced across that mysterious moon-drenched landscape.

If that howling pack of unholy beasts got in among our camp . . . There were women there, men who were representative of the gentle races of Kregen who wouldn't know which was the naughty end of a spear or a sword. They could all be destroyed, their throats ripped out, their guts torn and ripped bleeding from them . . . No. Oh, no. I couldn't allow that.

As the fleet zorca, a beautiful animal, bounded beneath me, I wondered anew over the problem of just how these werewolves kept making their appearance—and, always in my vicinity.

This was the malefic work of Csitra and her uhu, Phunik. Well, our two Wizards of Loh were hard at work trying to prevent this diabolical interference in the affairs of Vallia. Csitra might have taken a fancy to me; Phunik hated me, hated us all, both for the destruction of his father and for the wrecking of his insane ambitions to dominate all of Paz. If Phunik went the same road as his father Yantong we were in for another period of great distress, another horrendous Time of Troubles.

As that howling tide of gray horrors leaped on it, seemed likely that the Battle of Farnrien's Edge would be followed by the Massacre of Farnrien's Edge.

The women and camp followers, the servants and batmen, the grooms and cooks, would stand no chance at all when that ravening horde leaped upon them.

There are races on the bizarre world of Kregen who are not warriors, do not produce fighting men and women. The Relts, gentle-cousins of the Rapas; Xaffers, mysterious and distant; Dunders with their flat heads; ahlnims who are a race who produce mystics and wise men, all these and many more go about their daily lives while the world's stage resounds with the deeds of Chuliks and Khibils, with Rapas and Fristles. These people, then, were more than deserving of every effort to save them.

Fleetly the zorca galloped. She proved her quality on that night when the werewolves swarmed to attack the camp. Other zorcas stayed with us in the van. We were able to head the howling pack, to bear inwards, and then to ride alongside. Seg, legs clamped, was shooting already.

I used the ganjid-smeared dudinter blade. It was like slapping at a river in torrential flood. Grimly along the backtrail the corpses dotted the plain. We rode on, swords rising and falling, and the rout lessened.

At the last a few gancharks turned on us in a desperation that, I judged, came from their own natures and not the occult power impelling them. These we despatched. Only a scant three or four ran off, howling mournfully.

Seg shafted two, and a bunch of the lads rode after the others.

Our camp was in a frightful commotion; but men rode off to reassure the people. A deed had been done this night. Then began the grisly business of collecting the corpses. Well, there were men there I did not know, and others I did. This screeching pack of werewolves had been composed of men from many regiments. Some of them had blood on their lips; we suspected there was yet further horror to be discovered.

"There's just one good thing to come out of this night's work." Seg stood with me watching as the corpses were brought in. All of us bore faces like deathmasks.

"Oh?"

"Aye, my old dom. I've been expecting trouble among the troops. Mutiny. A lot of regiments were growing restive serving alongside the guard."

This I had suspected and dreaded.

Turko—wearing a dudinter sword—said, "Then whoever is doing these unholy things miscalculated tonight."

"We're all in this mess together, the guard, the regiments from Vondium, those of yours, Turko, those from Valka. If we fall apart now . . ."

"This fight has given us a real edge." Seg's fey blue eyes in the torchlight drove at me like twin lightning bolts, a stupid fancy; but exactly conveying the sensation. "Farnrien's Edge has given us an edge over Jhansi. I vote for an immediate forward movement of our whole force."

Our general growl of agreement was interrupted by the noisy arrival of a gang of soldiers dragging along two poor wights covered in mud and blood, their uniforms in tatters. When order was restored we understood that these two unfortunates had been discovered by the party who'd ridden after the escaping werewolves. The story was the same as that of Nugos the Unwary.

"You know what must be done." I spoke in that cold and hateful voice. By Zair! I was not a happy man in those dismal days. I took myself off and let other folk get on with the nasty business.

Passing a campfire I saw two of the Jikai Vuvushis clasping each other, sobbing their hearts out. I felt this was no business of mine. Whatever it was that was causing their distress—well, perhaps a quiet word with Marion . . .

She told me that, in the nature of things, liaisons had grown up between her girls and the men of their choice; strong affections—love, even—and that marriages were in prospect.

"But?"

"But, majister, many of the men they chose have been slain, some in battle, some turned into werewolves, some as victims of werewolves. I find it distressing—"

"Why have you not reported this before?"

"It is a feminine matter. I did not wish to burden you with unnecessary problems, seeing the many you already have."

She was quite right, of course. My Delia would have very quickly put me in order on that one. I bid Marion good night and went off to my tent.

A considerable quantity of bodies stood about my tent.

I sighed.

Each one of these fine lads and fair lassies was there personally to interpose their bodies between me and the enemy. Even if, as could easily be the case, the enemy was a horrendous ganchark. The thought that any one of those superb people could turn into a werewolf and rend the person nearby filled me with a hollow, aching passionate anger that was completely useless.

The habit of addressing a superior with "jis" for a man and "jes" for a woman was, as you know, increasing, paralleling the words "sir" and "madam" on Earth. These folk would call me majister if they were formal, majis if they knew me a little better. By the Black Chunkrah! My fine guard corps was being eroded, eaten away, destroyed by this occult and evil menace of the werewolves. It occurred to me that an expedition into the Snarly Hills of South Pandahem and a quick extermination of the horrors within the Maze of the Coup Blag might be an option I could not afford to ignore . . .

Just as I was about to flop down onto the spread furs, absolutely fagged out, a girl glided into the inner compartment of the tent. She was a Jikai Vuvushi I was more accustomed to see wearing her war harness, girded with steel weapons. Tonight she was half-dressed in a flowing rose-colored gown and bearing even more lethal weapons, not of steel. She carried a small hip-harp of eight strings and a pressel.

"May I sing to you, majis, for a short time before you sleep?"

I was too damned tired to argue.

"Very well, Floring. I am afraid I shall be a poor audience."

So Floring Mecrilli, a Jikai Vuvushi, a Sister of the Sword, struck the strings of her harp and played. She had a fine voice. I haven't the foggiest idea what she played and sang. The whole incident was unusual.

Presently she put her harp upon the rugs and, with a movement undulating and voluptuous, crossed to me and sank upon her knees. Her hair fell forward half-obscuring her face. Her dress was loose.

"If there is anything else I might do—"

"No, and I thank you, Floring. Now just let me sleep."

"If that is your command." She pouted. At once I felt alarm. "At least, for the love I bear thee, let me kiss you on the lips—"

I sat up, moved back and in a voice that might have blown out the gate of a fortress, said, "That is not for you, Floring Mecrilli. Now leave this tent—now!"

She flinched back. Her breast heaved with the suddenness of released passion. The single eye I could see past her downfall of hair looked glazed and staring. She licked her lips

"Please, my love—"

I jumped up, grabbed her by the shoulders, spun her about and carted her off to the tent flap.

There I placed her on her feet. I did not wish to shame her before her comrades.

"Now go out, Floring, and I shall forget this. If not, you are a soldier and are subject to the mazingle and strict regulations for all soldiers of Vallia."

With a final look, a look I swear was a startled look of self-revealed astonishment, she ran off. I went back to bed and gave her harp a kick on the way.

Just before I dropped off and thought of Delia, as I do on every single night of my life, I remembered my puzzlement over Khe-Hi's attitude when he talked of Ling-Li-Lwingling. Maybe romance was the cause of that, too?

Wizards and Witches of Loh spell their names as they please, and sometimes capitalize all three parts, sometimes not. There was no set rule. Capital letters at the beginning of words are highly erratic on Kregen. But, then, that mysterious and terrible world four hundred light-years from Earth is an erratic enigma at the best of times . . .

Perhaps only in the great word jikai are Capital Initial Letters of exact meaning.

Catching Khe-Hi at breakfast I tackled him directly.

"When I was down in LionardDen, known as Jikaida City, and fought in Kazz Jikaida, the game was controlled by Ling-Li-Lwingling as the jikaidasta."

"Yes, Dray. She is very good at Jikaida. The game has not, however, become an obsession."

I stared him in the eye, sternly. "She knew that I was from Vallia, and although I was called Jak I feel sure she knew who I was. Now I understand why."

He started to say something; but I went on, still fixing him with that baleful eye. "I believe you know that I bear you considerable good will, Khe-Hi. If there is anything I can do to further your—ah— relationship? romance? with Ling-Li—then for the sweet sake of Honeyed Soothe Herself, tell me!"

He did not exactly go cross-eyed; but he colored up—and he a renowned Wizard of Loh!

"I will tell you. Ling-Li traveled to escape the unwelcome attentions of Phu-Si-Yantong. One port of call was Jikaida City where you met her. She was, I can tell you, far more surprised to see you than you can imagine. She detested Yantong, and was happy to help circumvent his evil plans."

"So you knew I was there and just about alive?"

"More or less. We lost you for a space after that. Ling-Li went off to Balintol."

"And you? Look, Khe-Hi, I do not wish to interfere. But if you Wizards and Witches wish to remain a force in the world, it follows you must have families. So?"

"All right, Dray. Yes. I wish to marry Ling-Li, and I have high hopes she reciprocates."

"Well—go into lupu and see her and tell her to come to Vallia! By Krun! You know how welcome we'll make her."

"She has told me you were as hard as the granite of the mountains. That you did not bow the neck to her as any quivering frightened mortal man must before a Witch of Loh."

A sound that might have been a laugh burst from me. "By the suppurating armpits and vermin-riddled hair of Makki-Grodno!" I was very amused. "So your lady was offended by my uncouth ways. Well, I was in a fight—" I refused to think of the fight and of Mefto the Kazzur. "If she travels to Vallia she will be received with all the honor and respect due her. But, as you know, Khe-Hi, we do not keep slaves any more in Vallia."

"I will see what she says, Dray. And—I thank you."

Andrinos wrinkled up his foxy Khibil face. "My adorable wife, Saenci, has just presented me, as they say, with twins. Werewolves or no werewolves, San, I am glad to leave the horrific scenes of the night when feeding is due."

Turko finished swallowing a slice of roast bosk and remarked feelingly: "You may rail against the married state, Andrinos, my wrestling dom; but in me you see a pitiful object. A kov without a kovneva. A man without a helpmeet, a wifely companion, a warm snuggle at night. Well, then?"

Andrinos in the Khibil's superior way handled that with great aplomb.

"There are so many maidens, Turko, you cannot keep count. And now we have these Jikai Vuvushis, even on the battlefield you're at it, I know."

At Turko's astounded face we all broke into roars of laughter that, I fancied, were triggered as much by the desperateness of our situation as by true humor at Turko's amorous proclivities.

I said, "I had a visit last night from Floring Mecrilli who plays the harp and sings. I fear, pour soul, she is in great need, as dry as the Ocher Limits."

Turko quizzed up at this. "Plays the harp? Floring Mecrilli?" He reached for the first of the after-breakfast palines. "I wonder if the Sisters of the Sword have taught her aught of the martial arts? H'mm—I wonder, does she wrestle?"

CHAPTER TWENTY

AN OCCULT ROMANCE

Turko's Ninth Army of Vallia poised to strike directly at our foemen's capital city, Vendalume.

We were not a particularly strong army; but our formations were hardened, seared by the fire, still invigorated by victory. Layco Jhansi, renegade, would-be imperacide, murderer, traitor, was growing increasingly nervous and apprehensive at our attacks. No longer could he send with impunity columns to burn and sack the towns and villages of Turko's Falinur. He lost men in numbers to hurt him. He must have suffered desertions.

For our part when we captured a town or village, we did not burn it. Of course not. The place was Vallian.

Of the people who came into our protection those who were out-and-out mercenaries, paktuns who made a living hiring out as fighting men, were shepherded off to the coast and passages out and away from Vallia arranged for them. We kept no slaves; we hired no mercenaries. The code was harsh in Vallia on those subjects.

Of those who were civilians, we told them that they were first and foremost Vallians. They had mistakenly sided with Layco Jhansi because he was their lord. He was no longer the Kov of Vennar. He was outcast, leemshead. As Vallians we must create the island of Vallia whole once again. In view of my decision of the fate of Vennar, they would swear allegiance to Kov Turko as their new lord. Well, human nature is human nature; there were very few folk who felt that they ought still to cling to Layco Jhansi.

The knowledge that he had conspired against the old emperor, had willfully slain Ashti Melekhi, was a proven traitor, moved many of these folk. And, too, Turko's name bruited abroad as a kov at once firm but just gave them confidence in the future.

Good old Tom Tomor at home in Valka contrived to send to me another splendid regiment of Valkan Archers. He also said that he'd like to fly across and join me, whereat I had to be cruel and forbid him, saying that he ran Valka and that was his most important post.

Nath na Kochwold again raised the concept of bringing a Kerchuri down from the Second Phalanx in Hawkwa country. We were discussing this in a desultory way when the sky filled with wingbeats. We all looked up, standing outside the tents, shading our eyes, exclaiming in wonder and delight.

The two commanding officers of the two Valkan Archer regiments, Jiktars Fangar Emiltur and Nalgre Ephanion, laughed with the release of their hoarded secret.

"Tom Tomor bid us not to tell you, strom, for it was to be a wonderful surprise."

"It is," I shouted, elated. "It is."

Tom had sent across no less than five beautiful squadrons of flutduins, ridden by Valkans, highly trained, fiery of spirit, kings of the air. With these priceless reinforcements we could look forward to secure flanks as we advanced on Vendalume.

Khe-Hi cornered me later on that morning. Everywhere the camp resounded with the tinkering noises of men preparing for the great advance. The air misted with the campfires. The smells of cooking wafted on the breeze. And, over all, the Suns of Scorpio threw down their mingled streaming lights.

"Well, Khe-Hi?"

"Well, Dray. I have spoken to Ling-Li. I cannot repeat how it happened—"

I interrupted. "I assume she said something to the effect that she accepted my apology for my boorish behavior?"

"You know us too well, Dray!"

"Not quite. Not a Wizard or a Witch of Loh. Go on."

"She will come to Vallia." He looked down and while he did not shuffle his feet, for he was, after all, a very great sorcerer, he did wear the appearance of a wight in love. "And I hope, I have every hope, that she will, she will come to— that is—"

"Khe-Hi. You have my blessing and that of the Empress Delia. All that we can do, we will do."

"Thank you."

"How fared Ling-Li-Lwingling in Balintol?"

"Not well. They are indeed a strange people, all of them in that vast subcontinent. She has been in Pandahem."

I was not more or less just making polite conversation, for the welfare of all my people, including the Wizards of Loh, ranks high on my list and one is polite. In all our troubles the happiness of two people, a man and a woman, is and remains of supreme importance

"Interesting, for I was there recently, as you know. North or South?"?

"South."

I stared at Khe-Hi.

"You are working up to saying something, San. Spit it out."

"It is something you will not like to hear."

"Yes, well, I've heard a lot of that in my time."

"Ling-Li was not aware of it all; she warns me that she could be totally inaccurate. But she feels—"

"My dear San. If a Witch of Loh feels something, then, by Krun, that something usually *is*!"

"By Hlo-Hli, you are right."

"So?"

His red hair gleamed in the grateful lights of Zim and Genodras, his white gown, cinctured by the crimson cord, was spotless. His metallic voice took on a harsher ring as he spoke.

"What I propose must be done in secrecy. We must gather the Jikai Vuvushis, the Sisters of the Sword, who came back from Hamal with Marion and Strom Nango—"

I held up a hand. I felt a distinct pang.

"If what you are saying is sooth—and I see no reason to disbelieve you—we are, indeed, in evil waters."

"The Witch Csitra has planned well and cunningly."

"By Zair!" I felt awful. "I can only guess at what she has wrought. But she is in good case to destroy us."

"With the help of Ling-Li, of Deb-Lu, and of my own small powers, we can unravel the mystery. Then we may take steps to defeat her and her hermaphrodite child."

"Do what you have to do, Khe-Hi. I'll tell Targon

the Tapster and Naghan ti Lodkwara to afford you every assistance. Who else must know—apart from Turko and Seg?"

"It matters not who knows apart from Marion and her girls. It is sad, but—"

"Sad! It's heinous, diabolical, outrageous!"

"Yes."

"And this Hamalese, this Strom Nango ham Hofnar?"

"It remains to be seen how he will come out of this affair."

"You of all men, Khe-Hi, know how disastrous it is to attempt to fight thaumaturgy with a sword!"

"You can cut off a Wizard of Loh's head as easily as any man's if you catch the right moment." Khe-Hi lifted his upper lip. "I say this only because you already know it and because most people disbelieve it."

It would have been mawkish to have remarked on the other reason Khe-Hi could mention the fact.

Looking back at these events across one of the great watersheds of my life on Kregen, I must endeavor to place the alarums and excursions in their correct running order. These events formed links in a chain. If one was removed or misplaced the causality of the whole would fail. Already, from what Khe-Hi had told me, from my own observations here, my knowledge of Csitra and her hermaphrodite offspring, and the unpleasant results of all this occult scheming, I was partially able to grasp at the grand evil design.

That design was grand and it was evil; it was also simple. I didn't know it all yet; with the help of the sorcerers we would unravel all the twisted strands . . .

Of the survivors of the pastang from Marion's regiment cut-off in Hamal there remained only fifteen.

The others had fallen in battle, to our grief. One, Wincie ti Fhronheim, had returned to Vondium to have her baby in peace and quiet. The girls gathered in the tent put aside for that purpose. The canvas was surrounded at a discreet distance by a strong guard of 1ESW, 1EYJ, and by Sisters of the Rose, the Grand Ladies and other sororities in the Jikai Vuvushi regiment which, as yet, had no name.

"Where is Floring Mecrilli?" demanded Marion, who had—rightly—insisted on being present.

No one knew.

Khe-Hi pursed up his lips.

"No matter. We may proceed with those gathered here. Jurukker Mecrilli will be found when necessary."

So that meant there were thirteen Sisters of the Sword gathered to bear the scrutiny of a Wizard of Loh.

There was no doubt at all about it. Khe-Hi-Bjanching looked imposing, awe-inspiring, dominating the proceedings. About him clung that mystical aura of thaumaturgy that can shrivel the heart in the breast of the bravest.

He placed us in the positions he required us to take up.

The girls sat on folding camp stools in a semicircle. At the center Khe-Hi stood facing them. Each Jikai Vuvushi could see his face and look into his eyes. I stood at the back of the semicircle so that I, too, could look into his eyes. I knew what might follow if a mortal man looked into the eyes of a Wizard of Loh . . .

Slowly, Khe-Hi raised his arms. There was no mumbojumbo about a Wizard of Loh. He needed no arcane objects, no skulls, no morntarchs, no rattle of bones. He needed no fire stinking with incense. He had no requirement for Books of Power. Totally from within his own sorcerous resources, using the arcane knowledge painfully learned over the seasons and stored in his brain, he could draw forth the Powers he required and use them to awful effect.

Close at my elbow I could hear Seg breathing. This was unusual, hearing the hunter betray his presence. Seg was just as powerfully affected as I. Turko had flown off to inspect a churgur regiment, and on my other side Nath na Kochwold and Kapt Erndor stood, gripped like us all by the import of the moment.

Looking over the heads of the seated girls I became aware of a movement beside Khe-Hi. It was as though the air shimmered with heat. A second narrow column of disturbance grew into life at his other side.

I knew what this portended. The phantom shapes coalesced, thickened into the semblances of real live human beings. They were, indeed, real live human beings; but they were not physically present in the tent. They were miles away and by use of their kharrna they had gone into lupu and projected phantasms of themselves to join us in this weird interrogation.

At Khe-Hi's right appeared the familiar form of Deb-Lu-Quienyin. He could have been there in person, half-smiling at me, pushing his turban straight. I felt a great comfort at sight of his projected image.

At Khe-Hi's left shone the shape of a woman I had not seen since Jikaida City. She seemed to look the same, but her lupal projection was not as strong or as firm as that of Deb-Lu. Her red hair burned in the light from some source not confined within the tent. Her small face still looked as though it had been carved from finest ivory of Chem, unlined, smooth, with a firm compactness of flesh and distinct delineation of the lines of lip and jaw. Her blue eyes regarded me for a single glance only, still with that direct and challenging look. Then she devoted herself, as did the two Wizards of Loh, to the reasons she had projected her image here.

And yet—and yet in those fraught moments of high tension when everyone present knew that catastrophic events were to be unfolded, I caught the tiny interplay between Khe-Hi and Ling-Li. They were aware of each other. I saw that. Truly, this was an amazing circumstance for a plain sailorman like me! These two had carried out the rituals of courtship, they had plunged into romance separated by mile after mile of nothingness and yet still sundered by the truly vast distances of the world that separated them. They were involved in an Occult Romance— and I wished them joy of it.

Slowly, Khe-Hi brought his extended arms down. His hands passed through the phantom presences at his side. Now I could only look at his eyes. I was aware of nothing else.

From the eyes and brains of the Jikai Vuvushis, into the conjoined eyes and brains of the three thaumaturges, the pictures flowed, and so out again and into my eyes.

I saw.

The preliminaries had been done away with. We began in media res. A party of warriors huddled behind boulders, crouched low to the dusty ground. Spearing into the sky about them the jagged peaks of the Mountains of the West of Hamal leered down upon that desolate scene.

The wildmen crept closer, and shot and laughed, and dropped flat, taunting the Jikai Vuvushis.

The end was not far off.

The girls were hungry, thirsty, bloodshot of eye, and many bore wounds. Yet their spirit did not falter. They were Sisters of the Sword, and they would fight to the death.

Weirdly, to me, I recognized their faces. I knew them all, for in the present time they served as jurukkers within the guard corps. Jinia ti Follendorf stared around a boulder, her bow gripped, the last shaft notched. Hikdar Noni Thostan, the pastang commander, positioned at the center of that pathetic ring of defense, held herself ready to plunge to any threatened point, her sword clenched in a brown and dirty fist. Minci Farndion, not yet a Deldar, crouched low, ready to degut the first moorkrim to leap over her boulder. Floring Mecrilli was there, with two arrows left, and as I watched that scene she handed one of them to a companion whose quiver was empty.

Noni was the first to react to the eerie phenomenon. The viewpoint swiveled sickeningly and I was looking out across the scattered boulders, away over the evil slinking forms of the wildmen, up to a buttress of rock jagging from a sheer mountainside.

On that rocky shelf a light grew and blossomed.

I heard—or thought I heard—Seg gasp at my side.

The light expanded. The radiance soared from the cliff edge and sailed out over the rocks below. Now I could see a thronelike chair moving through thin air shimmering with uncanny power. Silks trailed from that throne and did not flutter in the wind of passage. Chavonth pelts and ling furs smothered the throne and steps in luxury. Rearing above the throne the jeweled canopy fashioned into the likeness of a dinosaur's wedge-shaped head seemed to glare down in demonic fury. The jaws gaped, the fangs glittered silver, and each eye was a vivid ruby furnace. Overpowering in effect, the throne and the risslaca canopy, sailing silently through the air.

Yet, all this was a mere frame for the woman who lolled in the throne.

Dressed in green and black with lavish gold ornamentation, she lolled with one white hand to her chin. Her pallor was intense. Her dark hair descended into a widow's peak over her forehead and swept in voluptuous tresses to her shoulders. Her green eyes regarded the scene beneath her, luminous slits of jade. Around her forehead a jeweled band held at its center a wedge-shaped reptillian head, jaws agape, scaled, ruby eyes malevolent.

Seg's hiss of indrawn breath was unmistakable.

"Csitra!"

The throne soared above the moorkrim. Two or three of those more brave or foolhardy than their companions chanced a shot. The shafts passed through the apparition. The woman's eyelids, coated in gold leaf, partially closed. Her mouth, a purple-red bud-shape, pouted.

The wildmen collapsed. They fell and lay in their windrows, unmarked, unwounded; but dead, all dead.

The Jikai Vuvushis stared up. No sound, no smell, nothing apart from the ghostly advance of the phantom throne and the Witch of Loh disturbed the mountains.

The whole scene fluctuated and wavered. I blinked. Black and red flashes of light and darkness slashed across like lightning upon a night of Notor Zan. The rocks, the mountains, the abandoned corpses of the moorkrim, the very throne itself, all shimmered as though seen through smoke or deep beneath the sea.

Csitra—if this manifestation was of the Witch of Loh of the Coup Blag—was putting forth occult energy. She had destroyed the wildmen for her own purposes; now she influenced the Jikai Vuvushis so that one by one they dropped upon the harsh ground, sprawling into the dust.

The vision faded, flickered—and was gone.

I came to my senses with the sounds of men and women coming alive about me, the smell of the tent and of oiled leather, the feel of sweat upon the air.

What we had witnessed was of immense importance. That would be investigated. I had the utmost faith in Khe-Hi and Deb-Lu. But there was a certain thing I must do . . .

Deb-Lu's image wavered as though he prepared to begone. Ling-Li-Lwingling's projection remained, and she half-turned toward Khe-Hi. I called out, harshly.

"Sana! A moment. We have met, as you will recall. I must tell you that you are heartily welcome in Vallia. I—"

"You have changed your tune, tiks—" she began to say, and then halted herself. Perhaps she had realized that as no one likes being addressed as tikshim— worse than our Earthly my man—thus to address an emperor in whose lands she might wish to live was little short of impolitic.

"Come to Vallia, Ling-Li-Lwingling. I hold Khe-Hi in the highest possible esteem. As for this Csitra—I can feel sorry for her, for she was enamored of an evil man."

"I will think on it, Dray Prescot."

Then, suddenly, like a smashed lamp, she vanished.

The Jikai Vuvushis sat on their seats like mice, hushed, shattered by what had been revealed to them, secrets locked into their unremembering memories.

Khe-Hi did not waste time on his own affairs. He said: "I believe I have the way of it now, Dray. I do not yet know the details of *how* it was done; but it is enough to know that it *was* done."

"Csitra bewitched the girls through her occult magic." I took a breath, feeling through all the evil horror the first hopes that now we could conquer the plague of werewolves. "They did not know—do not know. But it is they, the Jikai Vuvushis who survived in the Mountains of the West, who have been creating the werewolves."

"Yes. Without doubt."

"By the Veiled Froyvil!" burst out Seg. "*Turko*! I had an idea he wasn't inspecting that churgur regiment—and Jurukker Floring Mecrilli is not here! I'll wager—"

"That's Turko—and that girl tried hard to entrap me . . ."

We all rushed out of the tent. Turko! If we were right, and we knew we were right, then our comrade Kov Turko, Turko the Shield, was being transmogrified into a werewolf!

CHAPTER TWENTY-ONE

CSITRA'S PRONOUNCEMENT

"Kov Turko! Turko the Shield!" People rushed about the camp, shouting, yelling. "Jurukker Mecrilli! Floring Mecrilli! Kov Turko!" Everywhere men and women were running, ripping open tents, upturning carts, burrowing into piles of stores. The noise soared up to the suns. I was in a terrible state. Old Turko—turning into a ganchark! It didn't bear thinking of.

After I'd raced up and down yelling uselessly, I forced myself to calm down. This had to be thought out. A flutduin patrol was sent winging off to the churgur regiment out on the plain just in case Turko had really gone there.

Khe-Hi came panting up. "Dray, Dray! There is still a chance nothing has happened yet."

"What?"

"The stabs of occult energy. They must be the signals by which Csitra triggers a girl into action. I believe she bewitched the girls so that she could use her kharrna to spy through their eyes—"

"My Val!"

"—and when a victim and situation were ripe, she would order the girl to—"

"Do what, bite a chunk out of him—?"

"No, but—"

"Perhaps . . ."

I thought of what had happened. Of guards on duty kissing. Of the way Floring Mecrilli simply wanted to kiss me. Of the spots of blood on the mouths of men, caught as werewolves, who had not killed a victim. I thought I saw.

"Csitra peers through the eyes of a girl, sees a man, and then stabs her power. The girl and the man kiss."

"I will have all their teeth examined. It is known that teeth may be hollowed out and poison secreted. This will be no ordinary poison . . ."

"By Vox, no!"

"A bitten lip, a drop of blood, is that so unusual?"

Seg rushed by, yelling. "They think he took a voller! Come on, Dray!"

"Khe-Hi!" I fairly yelled. "Go into lupu and find him, and then tell us!"

"At once."

Even as Seg and I sprinted for the voller lines a ghostly figure materialized by the voller's chains, its turban toppling over one ear.

"He has gone to Gliderholme with the Jikai Vuvushi. There is a tavern there, The Sweet Gregarian."

"Warn him, Deb-Lu! Warn him!"

Deb-Lu's lupal projection wavered and vanished. Seg and I vaulted into the voller and the handlers cast off the chains. As we rose a frantic figure fairly hurled itself at the airboat. We looked over the side. Nath na Kochwold hung there, gripping onto a dangling chain, yelling blue bloody murder up at us. We hauled him inboard, and you may judge of our feelings when we made no uncouth jokes.

On that swift desperate flight to the little market town of Gliderholme which we had recently liberated from Jhansi's clutches, we tried to talk coherently about this affair and not to jabber mindlessly in anticipatory dread of defeat and Turko's ghastly death.

For, make no mistake, we knew what would have to be done . . .

"Hollowed-out teeth," said Nath. He shivered. "Well, how many teeth, then, per girl?"

We started to figure the computations.

"A damned lot," growled Seg. "Look at that howling pack after Farnrien's Edge."

"A lot of kissing went on then, that's for sure."

Other airboats fleeted after us. There was no further apparition either of Deb-Lu or of Khe-Hi. The air rushed past. We smashed the speed lever over to the stop. We roared on through the sweet air of Kregen under the twin suns, and we prayed to all the gods and spirits.

Although the ancients on our Earth speculated and the wise men of Kregen, also, had scientific and medical knowledge well beyond comparable levels on the Earth of that time, I was not fully aware of what a virus was or could do. Now I understand that Csitra employed the virus that caused the change in a man and turned him into a werewolf. The disease of lycanthropy, in which a person imagines himself to be a werewolf, must have played a part. The girl smiled and beckoned, and the foolish man succumbed, and Csitra watched all through the girl's eyes. A sweet kiss, succulent and juicy, and then the quick nip, the love bite, the token of passion. And, later, the awful change when Csitra willed, and the howling pursuit and the screaming and terrified victim . . . Yes, the Witch Csitra had gone great damage . . .

And those poor damned Jikai Vuvushis did not know a single iota of it all . . .

How Csitra must have laughed when they were incorporated into my guard corps. She could never have anticipated such a tremendous boost to her plans. And her plans had been working. She was quite clearly trying to alienate me. If wherever I went I was trailed by gancharks, the people would fall away, the fingers would point, there would be muttering, and dark looks, and then rebellion. She did not want to kill me, just to make sure I had no home in Vallia.

Her uhu, fruit of her unhappy liaison with Yantong, had quite other motives. Now I understood what Csitra meant when she spoke to me through the corpse of Larghos m'Mondifer. As a werewolf, Larghos had been impelled to attack me by Phunik. That could be the only explanation.

His mother still held power over him. While that situation lasted, I could feel a little freer. But, what when the uhu Phunik came into his own powers?

I had to look to Deb-Lu-Quienyin and to Khe-Hi-Bjanching. Also, with luck there would be Ling-Li-Lwingling to help. I trusted so.

"There it is!" yelped Seg. "There's the town. Now where's this dratted tavern?"

The thought of all that would be lost if we could not save Turko caused me to quiver as though straining against a dead weight. I thought of the times when Turko and I had escaped from the Manhounds, when we'd ventured down into Mungul Sidrath, of a score of adventures together, when we'd escaped from the wrestler's booths in Mahendrasmot. No! I wouldn't lose Turko! I couldn't!

Seg spotted the tavern by the sign. He simply slapped the voller down into the courtyard, thus smashing up one of Farris's fleet, and we leaped out, not stopping for the shouts and roared into the tavern.

Now Seg is a fine large fellow and the great lump of belly and chins that got in his way simply somersaulted out of it. Nath straddled the fallen man and we crashed up the blackwood stairs. Four doors at the top of the stairs, one half-open and so could be ignored. Three doors . . .

We each kicked one open.

The noise from below must be reaching up to the occupants of the rooms by now. Someone was going to go to investigate. The fates that run our lives, if such things as fates exist, sometimes smile and more often frown upon me.

A furred and feline Fristle swung open Nath's door even as he kicked. Then my boot crashed against my door and I went barging through. The fates, then, had selected me . . .

Turko, wearing a most fetching robe, was in the act of pouring a goblet of wine. The room was a simple tavern room with curtains, lamps, tables and chairs and a bed in the alcove. Upon the bed lay Floring Mecrilli wearing not very much but enough to maintain her estimation of herself and her decency. Turko looked up and the wine shot across the table.

"What the zigging hell!"

A scream of so rich and fearsome a quality burst from Floring that both Turko and I jumped to stare at her. She flung herself up from the bed, shedding draperies, her face ghastly, her eyes enormous, her forefinger pointing . . .

She pointed at the ghostly form of Deb-Lu who waveringly materialized at the foot of the bed.

"Khe-Hi!" came the faint voice of Deb-Lu. "Muster yourself, San, and quickly—"

Deb-Lu vanished.

Turko yelled: "What the hell's going on?"

I shouted: "Stand away from that girl, Turko, as you value your immortal ib."

Csitra, schemingly watching the scene through Floring's eyes, made her last cast. She knew there was but one chance; her stab of occult power penetrated the defenses woven by our two Wizards of Loh; but they were far stronger than she and would quickly annul her ascendancy.

Floring Mecrilli, a Jikai Vuvushi very quick and lithe, impelled by sorcerous powers, simply leaped on Turko.

He staggered back and yet, being Turko, one hand supported both himself and the girl around her waist.

"Throw her off, Turko!"

She did not kiss him. Like a snake she struck. Her mouth opened and a star splintered whitely from her teeth. She bit into his lips. Her head snaked back and blood glistened on Turko's mouth.

"By Erthyr!" yelled Seg at my back. I saw the point of a dudinter arrow appear at my shoulder, aimed at the girl, and as Seg loosed I struck the shaft up. It caromed away and smacked into the ceiling.

"What the—?"

"Look at Turko. The girl's part is over."

There was—as usual—the one slender chance.

By the kiss of dudinter . . .

Turko's transformation began to take place as Csitra's planning bore this evil fruit. Hair began to sprout on his hands, on his cheeks. He started up, and his eyes showed the horror dragging at him. I leaped.

The dudinter blade, smeared with ganjid, cut into his mouth. He tried to evade me, and I held him, I held a famed and feared Khamorro, and I cut into that bleeding lip.

Seg was there, gripping Turko, and Nath, too. We held him, and I cut his lip deeply, and dragged the flesh away, and then sucked and spat, sucked and spat, and shuddered deep into my vitals . . .

All this cutting and sucking and spitting is usually of little value; for the poison runs deeply and quickly. But the ganjid and the dudinter swayed the contest. Turko looked terrible. His eyelids closed and they were like overripe plums. He sagged in our arms. We carried him to the bed, stepping over the unconscious body of Floring on the way. We put him down and there was no need to send for the needleman, for Dolan the Pills who'd followed us in a voller, appeared, knowing he would be needed.

Critically we watched the hair on Turko's hands and face. Slowly, the hair vanished and he was our old Turko again. Dolan gave him one of his pills, as famed and feared as a very Khamorro himself, and Turko slept.

"By the Veiled Foryvil, my old dom. I'd not like to go through that again!"

"Nor, by Vox, would I!" quoth Nath na Kochwold.

"It would be best not to move the kov until he has rested," said Dolan. "But the girl had better be removed."

"It's not her fault," I said, somewhat harshly. "She must go back to her friends until we find a way to rid them of this curse."

A strong guard was posted on Turko's room, on the Sweet Gregarian, on the town of Gliderholme. When we reached the courtyard Oby stood contemplating the wreck of the voller, clicking his teeth against his tongue and fingering his chin.

"Some people," he said to no one in particular as we appeared, "should go back to learning to fly."

But he knew the score and simply expressed his feelings ellipitically.

"See what you can do, Oby. Turko is asleep and is our own Turko."

"Thank Opaz!"

During the next sennight as we finalized our preparations for what we hoped would be the final advance, news came in that the sorcerously duped people of Vennar were massing to resist us. Jhansi employed a certain Sorcerer of Murcroinim, one hight Rovard the Murvish. In his skins and bones, his leem-skull upon his head, shaking his morntarch, he conveyed the impression of a fearsome power. Also, he stank. The effluvium of rasts and sewers clung to him and preceded him by a goodly length of smelling range. He it was who overbore ordinary folk, turned them into screaming fanatics ready to fight until they were slain.

With Jhansi's regular paktuns leaving him, he had once again called on Rovard the Murvish for ungodly assistance.

Recovered, Turko had rejoined, and at this news he said, "I've had my belly full of sorcery. Let us go forward and blatter them. The Wizards, to whom I owe much, will do what they can. I do not think the issue will be in doubt."

"I agree," said Seg.

The coming campaign would not be easy, would not be a walkover. But we felt uplifted that we had removed the plague of the werewolves. The girls' teeth had been examined. They were not hollowed out. The virus, as I now know it to have been, had been precipitated by thaumaturgical art ready for use when the girl bit into the soft flesh of her lover's lip. The Wizards of Loh assured us the girls could be cured, completely, and could take up normal lives. At this we rejoiced.

Just before we were due to march and fly out, a voller winged in over the camp. We looked up and did not recognize her, although both Korero and Oby were confident she had been built in Balintol.

Khe-Hi started forward eagerly.

Well, yes . . . She looked as she had looked when she'd spoken so abruptly to me from the gherimcal upon the field of blue and yellows, just before that tremendous fight with Prince Mefto the Kazzur. Her ivory-smooth face, the level blue eyes, the piled masses of her auburn hair; all were as I remembered them. But, now, she stepped from the voller, inclined her head in greeting, and then walked swayingly toward Khe-Hi.

He looked radiant.

The Lahals were made, and everyone considered this a good omen for the coming campaign.

Khe-Hi said: "Dray. Ling-Li wants a private word as soon as possible."

"Of course. Oh, and when are you being married?"

"When you have heard what Ling-Li has to say, and decisions have been made, we will then set a date."

"Bad as that, is it?"

"Worse."

I refused to feel premature alarm. Seg, Turko, Nath and I went with Khe-Hi to this meeting with the Witch of Loh. Her tent was furnished luxuriously with her own belongings brought in her flier. She had a small retinue.

"Lahal, Sana. Tell us this dire news."

"Sit down, Dray Prescot. And the rest. Wine. Listen. I bear you no ill-will; I deprecate what I have to say. But if I am to live in Vallia with Khe-Hi, then I must do what I can to make my new home agreeable."

"A most sensible attitude," I said gravely.

She shot me a hard blue look that seemed to inquire if I mocked her. Taking up a goblet of wine, she said: "That is sooth. I have had a hard life. I was a pawn in the affairs of Phu-Si-Yantong and Csitra. But I learned. Khe-Hi and I have come to an agreement—oh, not in the flesh but through our own arts—and I feel confident I shall be happy in Vallia—if . . ."

I did not, and neither did my comrades, give her the satisfaction of idiotically mouthing: "If?"

She sipped. "You have penetrated to the core of Csitra's designs with the werewolves. You are just beginning."

Again we sat silently.

"Yes, Deb-Lu," she said on a sudden, dipping her head in a quick birdlike motion. "You may enter." Then, softening that haughty tone, she added, "You are very welcome."

The lupal projection of Deb-Lu glowed into phantasmal life within the tent.

"Khe-Hi said: "Tell us what you learned of Csitra's plans."

"Willingly. She has made a Pronouncement."

At this I saw Deb-Lu's hand go to his turban, and halt, transfixed. He stared anxiously at the Witch of Loh.

"With all due ceremony, with many human sacrifices, much shedding of blood, great agony of body and spirit, she has Pronounced the Curses."

We four mere men, not sorcerers out of Loh, listened to the Witch's words as she spoke on, and we listened numbed and drained and desperately concerned for the future.

"Occult forces have been stirred. Beings undisturbed for thousands of seasons have been roused. The reek of the ash pits, the screams of the dying, the long moaning wails of those in torment who may not die—all have been raised up against you. For the Witch of Loh, Csitra, has Pronounced the Nine Unspeakable Curses Against Vallia."

A silence followed. The tent's atmosphere cloyed. The two Wizards of Loh were overcome. Seg and Turko and Nath were unsure. Well, by Krun, so was I. But it was no good shying at shadows. I cleared my throat.

"Well, and, Sana. What does that mean?"

"Who can say what form the Curses will take? Werewolves—but of course! Vampires, and not the Vampires of Sabal, I can assure you. Plagues, famine, fires and pestilence. Infestation and Zombies and the Undead. Vallia has been cursed nine times. You may expect what you will receive."

I said: "On the morrow we march out to fight a great battle. After we have won that battle I will think what best to do about Csitra and the Nine Unspeakable Curses Against Vallia." That is what I said. What I thought was: "this sounds like it, Dray Prescot. I know what I'm going to do. I don't know what my Delia will say. I must take my chances and, perhaps for the first time in my life, go against Delia's wishes. But I know what I must do."

So we marched out to do battle with the traitor Layco Jhansi and his army of ensorcelled people, and, after that, as you will hear, I made my plans and proposed what I, Dray Prescot, would do. But, by the putrescent eyeballs and decomposing nose of Makki Grodno! What I proposed, what Delia proposed, and what happened, bore no relationship at all to one another. Not a single little bit, by Zair!

DAW

HEROIC FANTASY!

Do you long for the great novels of high adventure such as Edgar Rice Burroughs and Otis Adelbert Kline used to write? You will find them again in these DAW novels, filled with wonder stories of strange worlds and perilous heroics in the grand old way:

DAW

**Unforgettable science fiction
by DAW's own stars!**

M. A. FOSTER

☐ THE WARRIORS OF DAWN   UE1994—$2.95
☐ THE GAMEPLAYERS OF ZAN   UE1993—$3.95
☐ THE MORPHODITE   UE2017—$2.95
☐ THE DAY OF THE KLESH   UE2016—$2.95

C.J. CHERRYH

☐ 40,000 IN GEHENNA   UE1952—$3.50
☐ DOWNBELOW STATION   UE1987—$3.50
☐ VOYAGER IN NIGHT   UE1920—$2.95
☐ WAVE WITHOUT A SHORE   UE1957—$2.50

JOHN BRUNNER

☐ TIMESCOOP   UE1966—$2.50
☐ THE JAGGED ORBIT   UE1917—$2.95

ROBERT TREBOR

☐ AN XT CALLED STANLEY   UE1865—$2.50

JOHN STEAKLEY

☐ ARMOR   UE1979—$3.95

JO CLAYTON

☐ THE SNARES OF IBEX   UE1974—$2.75

DAVID J. LAKE

☐ THE RING OF TRUTH   UE1935—$2.95

NEW AMERICAN LIBRARY
P.O. Box 999, Bergenfield, New Jersey 07621

Please send me the DAW Books I have checked above. I am enclosing
$_____ (check or money order—no currency or C.O.D.'s).
Please include the list price plus $1.00 per order to cover handling
costs.

Name _____

Address _____

City _____ State _____ Zip Code _____
Please allow at least 4 weeks for delivery

DAW

Have you discovered DAW's new rising star?

SHARON GREEN

High adventure on alien worlds with women of talent versus men of barbaric determination!

The Terrilian novels

☐ **THE WARRIOR WITHIN** (#UE1797—$2.50)
☐ **THE WARRIOR ENCHAINED** (#UE1789—$2.95)
☐ **THE WARRIOR REARMED** (#UE1895—$2.95)

Jalav: Amazon Warrior

☐ **THE CRYSTALS OF MIDA** (#UE1735—$2.95)
☐ **AN OATH TO MIDA** (#UE1829—$2.95)
☐ **CHOSEN OF MIDA** (#UE1927—$2.95)

Diana Santee: Spaceways Agent

☐ **MIND GUEST** (#UE1973—$3.50)